Careful by the Railing

Careful by the Railing

George M. Taylor

Editorial Consultation: Dan and Dale Zola, Dan Coshnear, and Laurie Ann Doyle.

Graphic Consultation: Marc Takaha

Library of Congress Registration: applied for

ISBN paperback: 978-0-9644129-6-5
ISBN digital: 978-0-9644129-7-2

Audio Book and other information:
www.carefulbytherailing.com

To Debra

Chapter 1

The Wanderer

"How much did these boards cost?" Mr. Bello asked. He had come by to review Lou's work on a deck.

"You told me to get them at Home Depot." Lou knew where this conversation was going.

"Some of them are cracked already."

"You wanted cheap."

"You're wasting my money."

Lou's tools and orange power cords surrounded him on the worn deck. He wished Bello would get out of his truck when they talked.

"These loose railings are dangerous," Lou said. "All the steps and decks look this bad."

"That's my problem," Mr. Bello said. "When are you going to finish the other cabin?"

"You're going to have to pay me more," Lou said. He often had to hold his temper.

"Like hell I will," Mr. Bello said. "You know what we agreed to." He roared off in his big Chevy truck, towards the old, shingled house near the main road.

Lou put his pickaxe, pry bars and jackhammer back into the covered compartment of his truck. He slammed down the lid.

Later that evening, he sat with his neighbor Casey in the waning light, drinking beer. Redwood trees grew thickly on the steep slope behind the Orchard, a small community of summer cottages which had been converted into full-time residences.

"And look at my deck, falling down, too," Lou said as he finished his story.

"It must be tough to be the handyman here."

Lou grunted his agreement. "Where is Lily?" he asked. "I thought she was coming over."

"She forgot she had a hiking date with her flower club. Those girls, up and down the mountain. I can't keep up with them

1

anymore." Casey patted his left knee.

"Extra dinner for us," Lou said. After a pause, he continued. "I cannot keep Bello happy."

"So two years is long enough, for the wandering carpenter," Casey laughed. "I won't get too attached to our friendship. Last week the rats were gnawing... Don't get me started."

"It's life out in the country."

"I know. I just don't want you to go off somewhere else."

"Some day we will all be somewhere else, with Bello's property gone to hell. How long have you and Lily been here?"

"Long enough to see the place run down and you arrive, my friend." Casey clinked bottles with Lou. "The old man used to carry people. He knew he'd get his money eventually. Not Johnie."

Later Lou made chicken tacos for dinner, and the two men ate together on the deck.

"Every other month, Johnie wants me to work more hours, to pay off the rent," Lou said.

"He can do what he wants, since he's the owner."

Lou laughed. "I don't want any of your class war bullshit. I just want a fair job."

"Right."

"My old boss used to say, 'Don't start the job, till you know what the job is.' Well, I fucked that up."

"I cannot believe you ever worked for anyone," Casey said.

"I had to learn all these trades somewhere," Lou said, laughing. "Mr. Floyd. He was a drunk, but he knew how to put a building together. He went bankrupt in the end."

"Don't they all," Casey said. "Are you getting any sleep."

"Not hardly."

"Johnie?"

"No. Everything else."

In the springtime, a little creek ran through the back of the Orchard. Lou loved the sound it made as it trickled through the old apple trees and the run-down cabins. It had dried up now. A warm wind blew gently up the creek bed, and brought with it the smell of earth and redwoods.

His thoughts drifted out into the forest and up the hills on the other side of the creek. It went on for miles. The redwoods had been logged over two or three times. He loved the creaky whisper the tall trees made at night.

Stars came up over the dark ridge behind the orchard.

Lou thought, *it's so calm here.* He had his workshop nearby, and steady work.

"Are you listening, Lou?" Casey asked. He wiped his plate with a corn tortilla.

"Sometimes I think maybe it is time to move on."

"I know you are restless. Lily and I didn't go that way. A couple of kids make a big difference. What's that you're making?"

Lou looked down at his hands. He was whittling on a piece of oak branch.

"Looks like a little bird."

"Does it?" Lou put the carving down on the deck. He stood up and cleared plates off the little table. He rinsed the plates in the leaky sink. Then he sat back on his deck with Casey.

"All I know for work is construction. I see new places and do the same old things."

"You're like some Indian god, caught in the infinite loops of time."

"Back here again, for the first time," Lou said. "Life is good, right?"

Casey and Lou fell silent and drank from their beers.

At times like this, under the stars, listening to the occasional cry of the redwoods, Lou thought that maybe he could rest here in Bingo, that the forest could soothe him and help him forget his nightmares. He had lived in so many Northern California towns like this one. Maybe he was home.

Chapter 2

A Surprise Arrival

"Shit," Lou said when the chisel slid off the large owl he was carving, straight into his forefinger. With blood spurting, he slapped a rag on the wound, then rooted around in his shop for his first aid bag. While he wrapped up his finger, he looked at his shop full of carvings, and wondered how much of this art work he could take with him, when he left Bingo. If he could just find some place where he could sleep regularly.

Lou turned his bench grinder back on. Time disappeared, as sparks flew off his chisel, and he carefully watched the clean line of metal emerge against the dark brown of the spinning wheel.

He barely heard the insistent bell of his phone. He needed work, so he picked it up.

"Yeah?"

"Hey, mom's dead."

"Who is this?"

"Jennie. Who do you think?"

Lou took a deep breath. He hadn't been good at the long-distance relationship.

"Dad, you're as slow as ever."

"Where are you?"

"At the bus stop. I said 'Mom's dead.'"

"Dead."

"You flat-lining over there? I'm hungry. Are you going to come and get me?"

"Where?"

"Like I said. Bingo, the bus stop."

"Ten minutes."

"Bye."

Standing by his truck on the late summer afternoon, Lou felt the first cool wind of fall coming up the creek bed. Julie had died and he didn't even know. He felt lonely.

Was Jennie fourteen? Lou backed his truck out of the driveway.

When was the last time he had seen her? Some awkward birthday up on the North Coast.

No one waited at the bus stop. He parked on the street, got out and looked around. A tall girl carrying a large backpack walked towards him. Red tights highlighted her long legs.

"It's me, Dad. Goddamn it. You don't even know what I look like."

Tall, purple-streaked hair and angry. His Jennie?

"Ah."

"Yeah, I'm not ten anymore."

"You look…"

"Yeah. What?"

"Can we hug?"

Lou's arms wrapped around her camo-colored backpack. He smelled her and touched her for the first time in years. His daughter. He was still holding her when she pulled away.

"Where do you want to go?"

"After we get some food? Your house, I guess. You have a house, right?"

In the local burger shop, Jennie ate her salad quickly, and Lou noticed her mother's grey-green eyes. Julie was dead.

"She just keeled over, trimming bud in someone's shed and then…"

"Where were you?"

"Being homeschooled." Jennie made air quotes. "Mom had left me some pine cones and told me to study."

They both laughed.

"I found your number after the funeral. You disappeared like a ghost, or something."

Lou drank his water and thought for a moment. "Jennie…"

"It's okay. I need to get out of Paradise, too. Meet boys who don't talk about dope all the time. Go to a school with walls. Paradise is boring. Maybe Eve felt the same way."

"Eve?"

"Bible? Okay. Eve left Paradise. Hey, btw, my mom, your ex-wife, is dead. Like finito."

"Jen, all respect to the dead, she was gone when she was alive. Leaving you there was the hardest…"

"Fuck you. If you wrote once a year, I might believe you,"

Jennie said. She concentrated on her veggie burger.

Lou thought, *she's right.*

Then her tough-girl veneer collapsed.

"I miss her. I really do." A couple of tears filled her eyes. She stopped chewing and put her head down in her hands.

Lou reached across the table and halted the slide of her bright, purple-red hair towards the ketchup on her plate. He was supposed to do something consoling, but he didn't know what.

"You are fucking stiff as the boards you're always whittling on," she said, picking up her head. "I lost my mother. I have to stay with you. Like it or not."

"I'm sorry."

"That I tracked you down?"

"No, no. Jennie, this isn't easy for me either, okay?"

"Maybe you are human."

"I'm working on that. I like your hair."

"No, you don't. I stayed for a few weeks after the funeral. Never saw so many crystals and prayer beads. Now, here I am. Fourteen, full of burger and I stink. Can I go to your house now? I need a shower."

"Technically, you're a missing child. We should call…"

"I told Terry I was leaving."

"You stayed with them?"

"Who else? He was glad to get rid of me."

Lou looked out the window at the traffic. Jennie had come back into his life. Like some missing organ had been restored. He was a father again. Didn't he have enough problems?

Below Jennie's tough country girl was a winsomeness that Lou could feel. Her mother had the same quality. He had never been able to say no to it. Until finally he had to.

Chapter 3

At the Beach

"Is this what you do at the beach, just sit here?" Jennie asked. "I said you could bring a chair," Lou responded.

Jennie sketched a pair of gulls in the brown-white sand. Lou stared at her two-piece swimsuit. He couldn't get used to her. A young woman, with beautiful long legs. He couldn't believe how much she ate. How much she cost.

Four grey members of the pelican air force flew by in a perfect 'V' formation, a foot above the blue-green water.

Time passed. Water sneaked up on the sand, one ripple at a time, washing out Jennie's drawings.

Lou stared at the water and at the puffy cloud shapes which passed over the brown hills across the bay. This was his weekend. Quiet and smooth, or it had been until Jennie arrived. She rolled over on her stomach and groaned.

"Join those kids?"

"I'm too old for a fucking sand castle."

"Language."

"I'm practically an adult."

Jennie drew another big seagull. "She used to take me to the beach. Mom was usually so high, she couldn't get food for the picnic. I started shopping when I was seven... BTW, where were you? Fucking where were you?"

The kids digging in the sand turned towards Jennie's shouts.

She pushed her hands deep in the sand. "Goddamn it. I'm supposed to be over it."

She stormed off, and began skipping rocks over the blue-grey water, which the afternoon wind was stirring up.

Lou wondered, *Was he sad that Julie had died so suddenly, so young?*

He remembered the early days in Paradise. They had met local people who had plenty of work on their farms. Lou had always owned a well-tuned truck and showed up on time.

Lou and Julie had built a little shack in the hills, then added on a bathroom and a bedroom for Jennie. Julie had decorated it with weavings she had made from local wool. They had water from a spring, a wood stove, and a daughter.

Lou remembered carrying Jennie out on the deck to watch the stars come up. He sometimes carried her into the wild forest near their house and walked through the quiet moonlight, step by careful step. When he held her, a part of him felt quiet, like a red grey fox, which he occasionally saw at sunset. It was as if the forest entered him, deep inside. Then often he could relax and get some sleep.

Life with Julie had been good for a while, in Paradise. Then he'd realized that she was stoned all the time. Then the road had called. He remembered Jennie's face when he drove away from the cabin. He wanted to take her with him.

Did he miss Julie? No. Was he glad that Jennie was staying with him? Sometimes. Her moods.

"This is a prayer mandala," she said, pointing to an elaborate shape she had drawn.

"What's that?"

"Lou, is that you?"

Down the beach, a slim woman walked towards him.

"I'm April. You worked at my house last month."

"Hi. Can't see you." Lou blinked.

"Oh, sorry. Who's this?" April said as she moved out of the sunlight.

"Jennie, my daughter."

"Oh. Hi, Jennie. This is Yarrow, my son." A tall boy behind her, loaded down with a couple of bags, said hello without looking their way.

"Hi." Jennie didn't look up.

"Nice to see you," April said. "We're going down the beach."

After a moment, Jennie said, "She likes you."

"What?"

"Women know these things."

"Uh-huh." *My daughter thinks she's a woman,* Lou thought, amazed.

"That poor boy. Did you see his zits? He walks like he grew six inches in the last twenty-four hours."

Lou laughed. "Yeah."

"Oh god, he's coming back."

"Ah, excuse me, sir. April asked me, I mean Mom, I mean asked me to ask you... Can you help me? We bought a kite and, ah..."

"Sure, bring it over."

Lou reached into his duffle bag and pulled out his pocketknife. "Jennie, did you put in the sandwiches like I asked you?"

"You didn't ask me."

"Okay. We don't have any food. Only a couple of bottles of water."

"Whatever. We passed a store back there on the road. I knew it. They are both coming."

April carried a box with sticks and string falling out of it.

"I think I bought two kites," she said when she handed the box to Lou. "Without knowing it."

Lou stared at the box for a moment. "Yarrow, is that your name?"

"Uh, yeah."

"Want to help me?"

"Okay, but I..."

"Are you going to Bingo High?" April asked Jennie, as Lou and Yarrow worked on the kites.

"I guess," Jennie said, rolling over on her stomach.

A few minutes later, Yarrow and Jennie ran down the beach through picnic blankets and yelling happily. The brightly colored kites cut through the blue sky.

"Nice work, Lou. I didn't know you had a daughter."

"I didn't either. That didn't come out right. She lived with her mother, so I haven't seen her much."

"I like her. Is she visiting or staying?"

"I don't know."

Lou fell quiet. His uncertainty sounded weird to him. April wrinkled her brow. Maybe Jennie was right. Something in April was pulsating at him.

Sometimes it seemed to him like the whole world was coming at him in a crazy chaos of colors and sounds. If he could just focus on the incoming tide licking at the shore, or on the sea gulls tearing into someone's lunch bag, if he could focus on just one thing, he would be happy. He could rest.

He knew that was why he liked wood carving so much.

He was happy with April sitting next to him. Yarrow and Jennie dropped their kites in a pile and swam out to the raft together.

Jennie pulled herself up on the raft with one clean yank, while Yarrow struggled with the short ladder. A few minutes later, they were standing up, and balancing on the raft which rocked with the incoming tide.

"You know what's coming," April said.

Suddenly Jennie lunged at Yarrow and pushed him into the water. Yarrow climbed out and returned the favor. They lay on the raft for a while, then they were pushing each other again. They both rolled into the water.

The sound of Lou's and April's laughter joined and went out over the bay towards the blue sky and their children.

Lou didn't know where he was going to live, or if Jennie would stay with him.

For a moment, life was good. He could relax. Everything that was coming at him hadn't happened yet.

The afternoon wind drove the waves up onto the beach. A family to their right moved their blanket farther from the water.

Jennie ran up on the beach with Yarrow behind her. "Yarrow touched me." She looked upset.

"You attacked him."

"No, on the raft he grabbed my...my...you know." She clutched her chest with both arms.

Yarrow turned red and said, "That's not what happened."

Lou looked at April and said, "I have no idea how to be a parent."

"Join the club," she said. "Do you want a sandwich?"

Chapter 4

Mrs. Goodwin's Plumbing

A broken screen window sat next to a dried-out fuchsia on the porch. Lou knocked on the door of Mrs. Goodwin's house.

"My sink is still leaking," she said as she opened the door. "I paid you to fix it."

"Right. Hello, Mrs. Goodwin."

Lou entered a small living room that smelled of plants and mold. He knew this was going to happen.

"I cannot afford poor workmanship. If my son were still alive, he'd have fixed it right." Mrs. Goodwin's anger was ruining the small bit of calm which Lou had felt while drinking his coffee, after he'd gotten Jennie off to school.

"Plus, I have to clean up the sink to let you take a look at it, and that takes me a long time. The housekeeper, who can't work worth a lick, isn't due for ten days. You better fix it this time."

"I'll get my tools out of the truck," Lou said.

"Don't be snappy with me, young man."

I don't need this kind of shit, he thought.

He did need the money.

Lou took cleaning fluids, old sponges and rags out from under the sink and carefully put his head in. He knew what he would see.

Mrs. Goodwin calmed down and asked, "Do you want some coffee?"

"Sure." Lou sat down at a rickety kitchen table with her.

"Well?"

"The new faucet doesn't leak."

"So you say."

"I told you re-caulking the sink wouldn't work."

Mrs. Goodwin put her cup down, and the table swayed a little. "That conversation never happened."

Lou said, "How do you make such good coffee?"

"Don't try to distract me, young man. I've lived in this house a long time, and everything is breaking."

Looking around the old kitchen, Lou saw black and white photos hanging off the refrigerator, affixed with yellowing tape. A 1950's-style blender sat on worn black and white tiles. On the tops of the cabinets sat large old pots, ancient tool boxes and three long fluorescent light fixtures.

"I haven't touched that stuff in years," Mrs. Goodwin said. "So what? Now can we talk?"

"Sure." Lou hadn't mentioned his customary fifty-dollar minimum for a house call.

"Oh, the sun is out. Let's go out on the porch." She rose slowly from her wooden kitchen chair. "Bring your coffee."

She walked out the back door to a couple of worn wicker chairs on a brick patio that overlooked her yard.

"Don't look at the garden. It's embarrassing. We used to eat tomatoes, cucumbers. Oh, what's the use." She sipped her coffee.

"Mrs. Goodwin, I'll re-caulk the sink for free. But you'll just have to keep wiping up water underneath until you get the sink leveled and re-tiled."

"I'll be dead before I can afford that."

"Look, I'll come back if you need me." He started to get up.

"Hey, finish your coffee."

He had another job in the afternoon, but sat back down.

"I won't bite your head off. I'm too tired."

She looked out at the garden for a moment and smiled. Her face relaxed and Lou noticed the vitality in her blue eyes. She was going to go down swinging.

"We used to fight off the deer with fences, with piss smells in spray bottles. Finally my husband shot a couple. No matter how high we built the fence, they got in. You could probably handle that better than Wally."

"I've built a few."

"Don't get your hopes up, Lou. I'm not hiring you."

The sunlight and the faint ripple of the wind through the trees pacified Lou.

He could re-caulk the sink in less than twenty minutes, and it might hold a while. Maybe not. Sink water puddled and drained down into the lower cabinet.

"After San Francisco, Wally and I wanted a small town,

wanted to know the people around us. We raised our kids in a quiet neighborhood. I guess that worked out, but Frannie left. Then Terry. He died in Iraq. For what?"

She was quiet a while. "Frannie calls me once in a while. All the neighbors left, too. Hey, I have no regrets. I eat, I have a roof, and I have…"

She stopped talking and sipped her coffee.

"I never had that kind of stability," Lou said.

"I can tell."

Listening to her, Lou felt something tug on his heart. Sometimes he felt superior to all the people he saw, rushing around in their vans full of kids. Like he was more peaceful, open, in the flow. Other times like now, he wondered why did he always want to be somewhere else.

Lou put his empty cup down and went in to fix the sink.

Later, at lunchtime, he met Casey in one of the small parks near the downtown shopping area. Under some small redwoods, he unwrapped a sandwich and offered another one to his friend.

"I'm not hungry," Casey said.

"I can eat it later."

"Lily fell on a hike. She may have hit her head.'

"Shit."

"We're going in this afternoon for a check-up."

"That sucks."

"She broke the 'no-falling' rule. Of course, I'm worried. What have you been up to?"

"Mrs. Goodwin's house. That tough old lady. She knew how to go after what she wants. I never learned that."

"You still might. You're young."

"Her dream was to come to Bingo and stay. Now she's up there in the hills, all alone. Does she feel successful? Or bitter?"

"Maybe both," Casey said. "Depends on the day."

"I got to get back to Lily," Casey said. "Let's do this again, Lou. Next time I'll be hungry."

Chapter 5

Beautiful Music

"When the water from the leak spread onto that rug, his old piss really started to smell," Aaron said. Reaching down from his wheelchair, he petted a sad-eyed Bassett hound.

Lou looked at stacks of shipping boxes, piled six or eight high, all the way around the small living room. He smelled mold, old paper and dog. He had come to Aaron's battered cabin to make repairs and to visit.

"After my death, I'll be discovered as an authentic nobody from the Midwest who heard America calling and tried to write the song of these states down in prose."

"Aren't you misquoting..."

"Ginsberg. He said he'd introduce me to Ferlinghetti, but then he sobered up. He never sent back a box of my writing. The cheap prick."

Lou moved a stack of papers tied together with a rope and started to sit down.

"Whoa, careful. That's my twenty-third novel."

Lou picked up a few loose pages off the floor while he found another chair.

"I think Bassett peed on that pile over there too. Smells like it. Critics say that writers ossify. Ossify means 'bone,' you know. Maybe my talent turned to bone, as in boner. There's a theme you could build a novel around."

Aaron muttered, "Sex, two men, dog." He made a note in a loose-leaf binder on the battered table next to him. At least ten other binders lay on the floor near Aaron's wheelchair.

"I read that if you wrote a million words a year, you'd be rich and famous. That's not my goal, of course. Now that I can't afford paper and ink."

"I'll buy you supplies."

"Kind of you. Writing in my head saves trees. I can recite my novels, if you ever have time to come by. Like *Fahrenheit 451*."

"I liked what you read at the open mike."

"That was eighteen months ago. Deferred gratification. A writer's life story. I'm not writing for posterity. Those assholes who control publishing. *Posterity* has the same root as *posterior*, you know? Something behind you."

Lou thought for a moment about everything he had behind him. Then he looked at his watch. "Ah, can we..."

"What's your hurry? I'm not going anywhere."

"It's a workday."

"That means you are carving some endangered lizard... Oh, don't look at me like that. I know you need to make a living. I bought this moldy, falling-down cabin with my mother's money. I hated her. Glad she shuffled off this mortal coil. Love her money. Everything I write is about her and my dad. When I inherited their furniture, I burned it all. The day of his funeral. A Viking ritual. I almost burned down the house that day. That's how I wound up in the chair." Aaron patted the metal wheels.

"I'd like to burn my father's furniture and him tied to it," Lou said. "But that's another story."

Aaron continued. "Oh, a little rage. You can tell me about him some other visit. I've got time, Lou. If hours were money, I'd be rich. Well, I am rich. But cheap. I thought you'd understand. See that folder over there? That story went off to The New Yorker in '87. I never heard back. I'm still revising it. A person who needs the promise of fame to write isn't an artist. You know what I'm talking about."

Aaron smiled beatifically and looked at his bookshelves. "There's beautiful music in my head all the time. You can burn my written legacy with the rest of my parents' furniture. Americans are not ready to hear their own voice, their own song. I hear it, tied to this chair, imagining what's happening right here in Bingo. There is so much pain and love. Wow, there's another novel." He scratched a few words in his binder.

"But that's enough about me, Lou. When you first moved here, I thought you were like a ghost ship way out on the ocean."

"Okay."

"Maybe because you are so pissed off. I knew you were coming from somewhere, but you didn't know where to land. Then you told me that you made wood sculptures. I understood.

Then I could write about you."

"Me?"

"Of course. Me and Proust, we write about everything. His biggest mistake was writing in French. Who reads French anymore? My analyst said my writing was all about my parents, but fuck him. He committed suicide just before we got to my mother complex. I could have been cured. My theory is that you don't really exist until I write about you."

"Wow. Do I exist when I go home and feed Jennie?"

"Not for me. Jennie who?"

"My daughter…"

"I have to think about that." Aaron took a note. "Great. Another novel is born."

"She's fourteen. Everyone says going on thirty but I can't say it."

"Why not?"

"She's still my little girl."

"Well, sure. Mine is forty-three. I still think she's going to climb up in my lap. Daughters."

"I should do your plumbing job before lunch."

"What's your hurry? I need to talk to you, so I can bring you into focus."

"April said the same thing."

"Another daughter?"

"She's a woman, actually. She wants to be my girlfriend."

"Oh," Aaron said and smiled. "She wants you to talk to her."

Lou smiled. "How did you know?"

"She wants to know where will the ghost ship wash up. She's asking the wrong guy. How would you know?"

"Right. Once you leave your hometown."

"Listen to me, Lou, " Aaron interrupted. He looked down at his wheelchair and shrugged. "Don't be bitter. You are an artist. You will never have a home."

Lou looked around at the ramshackle house of his friend, at the collapsing bookshelves, at the piss-filled boxes and, finally, at the thin, bent-over man in the wheelchair.

"I'll never leave my house," Aaron said, patting the wheels again. "But I wouldn't trade my life for anyone's."

Chapter 6

A Close Brush with Intimacy

"We made it happen," April said.

"You did," Lou corrected. They stood in line at Coffee Heaven, on the corner where Bingo's two commercial streets crossed. Five weeks after the beach encounter, April had arranged a coffee meeting. Fall's morning sun slanted through the tall windows.

"Two working single parents," April said.

"Takes some scheduling."

Some bond, Lou thought. They collected their order and sat down at a small round table.

"Do you have to wear your shades?" April asked, as she put her tea down.

"Sorry," Lou said. He shifted around the little round table a few degrees.

"Now I can see your eyes."

"Are you used to people lying to you?"

"I'm a high school counselor."

"Jennie hasn't learned that skill yet."

"Right," April said. "She's a teen."

Lou drank his coffee and noticed Casey reading the Chronicle at the next table. He waved and asked, "How's Lily?"

"Not so good." Casey looked back at his paper.

"You know a lot of people."

"I've been doing odd jobs here for two years."

"Do you know me?" April stirred a packet of sugar into her tea.

Lou looked away. Daylight was burning up, and he had another mouth to feed. Was April coming on to him? Or was this some of her counseling bullshit, guiding a conversation while she nursed her private thoughts?

She was nice to look at, slim, dark-haired. Her eyes had an engaging vitality. Lou looked around the café.

"Now you're pulling back a bit. Unused to the attention?"

"What are you... Never mind." Lou couldn't tolerate such directness without his morning coffee. He chewed his cinnamon roll and said, "Don't you love sugar?"

April continued. "In the pauses in our conversation, I could do a crossword puzzle."

"Not a hard one."

Lou laughed. "Okay. I'll share. Once you live way out in the country..."

April laughed. "I knew it. You were raised by coyotes."

Lou laughed again. "Yeah, I learned English a few years ago." He took another bite out of his cinnamon roll.

"I will get a crossword puzzle," April said. She looked around the café. "Do they sell the paper here?"

"I thought you'd get all soft and fuzzy if I shared something with you."

April leaned towards him and blew on her tea. "Is that what you did?"

"Telling you I was raised by coyotes? That doesn't count?"

Lou said hello to another coffee drinker who stepped by their little table.

"I feel a kind of inner tension here in Bingo. I don't know if it's mine or..."

"Do I make you nervous?"

"Everyone's in a hurry. In the country, there wasn't so much to do."

"You think my biological clock is ticking. Is that it?"

Lou decided to settle down. What was there to fight about?

He sipped his coffee, then said, "I'm not explaining well. Something in the redwoods, something wild in the ocean when I was surfing, settled into me. Farming, watching crops grow. Hiking deep into the redwoods. I find it soothing. Like sitting here drinking coffee with you. It's slow. But look around. All the gadgets. It's like everyone in here is waiting for the next call, next text, next thought."

"That's deep. The line about the thoughts."

"I read a book on Zen once. Do the people in here look happy?"

"Aren't you the guy who cannot settle down?"

"Who told you that?"

"Maybe I guessed it. Growing up in the city, I don't really know what you are describing. Where is this silence? Can you take me to it?"

"Now? It's not like a pill."

"How far would I have to go?"

Casey leaned over from the next table. "Lou, just take her out to the meditation center in the valley and drop her off. I'm Casey by the way, Lou's neighbor. I can't help but overhear." Casey reached out to take April's hand.

"*Eavesdrop* is the correct word," Lou said.

"Okay, okay."

Casey shook hands with April and started to return to his newspaper.

"Wait. What meditation center?"

"Goodbye, Casey," Lou said.

"I can take a hint," Casey growled. He turned away.

"No. Stay. How far would I have to go?"

"You'd have to go all the way," Casey said.

"Wow, do you always speak in riddles?"

"I try to string out my conversations, because I don't have many of them. I'm out on my own now for an hour or so, then I have to get back."

"His wife fell," Lou said.

"I'm so sorry. Is she all right?"

Casey looked around the café. "You said you want to know what silence is?"

"I think so."

"It's sitting there in your little house, watching your wife breathe. She was healthy, then she fell, now she can't breathe. Sitting there in the morning, watching the light come up on the wall over her bed. Listening to her breathe with the mask on. Hoping she takes the next breath. Hoping you can tell her that you love her and you had a good life together. That you're sorry for all the shitty things you did. Then there's a small space between the inhalation and the exhalation. It's a silence so full of life, it could break you in half."

"I don't know that kind of silence," April said. "I don't."

Casey looked at her kindly. "Trust me, young lady. You don't want to."

Chapter 7

Lou's Gay Neighbors Fighting and...

"It's so hot," Jennie said. "Plus, I've got homework. This crazy math." She was sprawled out, long legs akimbo, on the floor of Lou's little living room. Around her, a paper snowfall of graphs and charts.

"It'll be cold soon enough," Lou said. Sitting at the kitchen table, poring over an estimate, he felt so tired.

"I remember rain, FYI," Jennie said. "Every fall, in Paradise."

"Do you ever want to go back?"

"Hold on a second." Jennie closed her book with a snap. "Do you?"

"Just thinking out loud."

"Well, don't."

Lou crunched numbers for a few minutes, then said, "We told Freddie and Tommie we'd be there for lunch."

"No, you told them. I'm not some little doll you can trot out in public, you know."

"I asked you a week ago, then again last night. Look, there's nothing in the house to eat."

"There's a good argument. Did you tell them about my diet?"

"Which one?"

Jennie smiled, "Okay, I'll make do. Plus, I can delay my math ordeal. Will you help me?"

"I told you. I don't do geometry."

"Did you flunk it?"

The previous night's shower had cleared the air, and the sunlight was dazzling. Lou walked through wet maple and oak leaves on the path to his friends' house. He noticed how the landscaping had been carved out of the surrounding redwoods, which climbed densely up the steep hill behind the Orchard. Sometimes Lou's life seemed squeezed by the trees.

Jennie waved her phone in the air. "Crappy reception but better than Paradise."

"Careful by the railing," Lou said, as they walked up onto their friends' porch.

"Hello, hello, hello," Freddie said. "Charming, simply charming. And this must be Jennie. I've seen you around, of course."

"Must be," Jennie said.

Lou got a little more tense. "She meant 'hello'."

Freddie ushered his visitors inside. His partner, Tommie, a large man in a checked cotton shirt, got up slowly from an overstuffed leather chair.

"Freddie, these chairs are so uncomfortable."

"You're getting old, sweety."

"This looks like a warehouse," Jennie said, looking around at several of the chairs, four ancient standing lamps, and several marble-topped tables with carved legs.

Lou glanced at her, and she continued. "I mean, a cool retro warehouse."

"I'm sure," Tommie said. "We like what we sell."

"Thanks for having us," Lou interjected. *How do you parent a daughter who speaks her mind,* he thought.

A small barking dog began humping his leg and barking.

"Down, Frederick, down," Freddie said.

"I know that bark," Jennie said.

"You said you would train that beast, honey," Freddie continued.

"Work in progress," Tommie said. His huge forearms stuck out of his plaid Pendleton.

Lou calmed down when Jennie said, "I like dogs, especially if they stop barking."

"Well, that might happen," Tommie said. "Come here, Frederick."

All four sat down in the living room, with the little dog on Tommie's lap.

"Frederick the Great is his full name. Oh, how nice that he stopped barking, barking," Freddie said. "How we got him is such a story."

"Oh, they don't want to hear it," Tommie said. "Down, boy."

"I love your tie," Jennie said to Freddie, who wore a light blue ascot that matched his eyes. She drank her grape juice.

"Let's talk about food," Tommie said. "I have a leg of lamb. Then your father, such an artist but not good with food choices, said that you were a vegan. Tell me, dear, what exactly is that?"

"Oh, I love lamb," Jennie said. She crossed her legs and sat up straight in her overstuffed chair. "Do you have really large guests? This chair..."

"Oh, I know, dear," Freddie said. "Tommie had to have it."

"Stop it, Freddie. It's the Funktique look," Tommie said. "Plus, I am large. You might have noticed."

"Well, I did," Freddie said. "I sure did."

"Funktique?" Jennie asked.

"Our store in town. You must have seen it."

"Ah, no. I let Dad buy the furniture, which he does every decade or so."

"She is so clever," Freddie said. "There's just a little much of it here, don't you think? Always I'm stumbling."

Tommie continued. "You said you wouldn't fight when the guests were here."

"I'm not fighting, just expressing myself," Freddie said.

Tommie turned towards Jennie. "We love to fight and ... Oh never mind, dear. You are too young."

"I know the expression," Jennie said. "I lived on a ranch with my mother. We saw a lot of that, you know. Bulls, goats. They all did it, right in front of me."

"How exciting," Freddie said.

"Yeah, we slaughtered lambs. I did it once. You cut their throats and hang them upside down till the blood drains out."

"How horrible. Have a cookie," Freddie said. He took a wooden tray full of oatmeal cookies off the table next to him. "I made them."

"I lost the annual sacrificial lottery," Jennie said. "That's why I left. A crowd was chasing me."

"What? You lost me," Tommie said. He brushed a cookie crumb off his shirt.

"They were going to cut my throat," Jennie said. "It's a community ritual."

"Didn't I read that book in high school?" Freddie asked.

"Ah, joke," Jennie admitted.

The two men laughed, and Freddie said, "I love your hair, by the way."

"Thanks." Jennie brushed the purple-red locks back from her face.

"Lou looks happier since you came," Tommie said.

I do? Lou thought.

"Even though we love our rustic quarters here, we're really city people," Freddie added. He held Tommie's hand. "It's safer for us."

Tommie nodded and smiled. "I was attacked viciously in San Francisco. My boyfriend died then."

Jennie touched her heart. "I'm so sorry."

"Mine died in the AIDS crisis," Freddie said.

"You are such a drama queen," Tommie said.

Freddie went into the kitchen, and Lou relaxed.

After dinner they ate homemade berry pie out on the back deck. Lou looked out at the redwood forest across the creek. On the weekend, he could relax. A happy lunch on the deck. Warmth, inside and out.

He liked the Orchard, the sense of community. Of continuity. Jennie clearly delighted his friends.

"You know about Achilles and Patroclus, right?" Jennie asked. Lou caught her eye and wiped his lips with a forefinger. Jennie used her napkin on a blueberry stain.

"A new SF restaurant," Tommie said. Frederick was perched quietly on his lap.

"No silly, The *Iliad*. Tell us, dear. We love stories."

"It's a long story. The Greeks go to Troy to fetch Helen. The Trojans want to keep her. Achilles almost dies of sorrow when Patroclus is killed fighting. They are lovers, according to some traditions."

"Of course, dear. We knew that," Freddie said.

"What is the EEliad?" Tommie asked.

"It's the only gay epic, dear," Freddie said.

"Don't condescend."

"Achilles pouts after an argument with Agamemnon and won't fight the Trojans. Patroclus borrows Achilles' armor, but he, Patroclus, advances too far into the Trojan army, then is killed by Hector. All the heroes are related..."

"Kind of like Bingo," Freddie said. "Patroclus would be

Tommie, if this were an allegory. He's such a warrior. He fought off the Aryan punks who attacked him and Richard. Are you studying this in school?"

"Homeschooling, this was my favorite story. For a long time, I thought I was gay. We had a graphic novel of *The Iliad*, our only book. My mom didn't read much."

Frederick started barking and Freddie said, "Now Frederick the Great wants us to tell his story. It's our own private myth, you could say. Dare I?"

"Of course."

"Jennie, you look like you need another piece of pie."

Jennie looked at Lou.

"Why not?" he said.

"Don't you mean 'pie not'?" Jennie punned.

"Frederick is not named after me," Freddie said. "The dear boy already had his name. We added 'the Great.' Jackie, that was my precious previous husband, had finally died. Day and night I nursed him for four torturous years. The ups and downs."

"The dog story, please," Tommie interrupted.

"This is part of it, don't you see. The death devastated me. Finally, I came out of my grief and what was I going to do, date? I don't think so. I wanted someone, something, to hold, to talk to. So I went to the Humane Society. Every week for months."

"It was harder for me," Tommie interrupted. "To lose Richard in the attack. The beasts almost tore my head off and I had a headache for weeks. Such a sudden loss, like my heart had been ripped out of my body."

"No doubt the long, slow route is worse, the emotional wear and tear on me," Freddie said.

"What do you know?" Tommie started to cry. "Why do I have to convince you that my loss was worse? You just won't admit it. You knew Jackie was going to die and you got ready. You were lucky."

"Lucky? I won't have this. Do you think I sealed over my heart all those years? No. It was wrenching."

By this time, Tommie and Freddie were standing. Tommie was crying and yelling, Freddie just yelling.

Lou tilted his head towards the steps, and Jennie followed

him. The two men paid them no attention as they continued to shout at each other.

As Lou and Jennie walked back to their house, Jennie asked, "Was that foreplay?"

Chapter 8

Lou's Pet Coyote

After their dinner at a Pan-Pacific-style restaurant in Bingo, a walk brought April and Lou to his little house on the edge of the woods. The fall stars started to shine as they left the soft glow of the town lights.

Lou loved night in the Orchard, with the forest and the dark pressing up against his cabin. He felt held by the wilderness in a way that soothed him. He wasn't sure April would understand.

"Hey, this is nice," April said, as she entered Lou's cabin for the first time.

"You think so?"

Lou looked around. He had cleaned up, hoping that April would come home with him. The little cabin was shabby. Worn. And Jennie's stuff had begun a relentless invasion. Her Bingo High sweatshirt, laptop, and schoolbooks were strewn on the little dinner table.

"You keep it aired out."

"You think it's cold."

"I like fresh air."

"I don't like to be inside much," Lou said. "Do you want me to close the doors?"

"I didn't know you were a reader," she said, nodding towards the floor-to-ceiling shelves full of paperbacks.

"All repair manuals," Lou said, laughing.

"Ananda Coomaraswamy," April said, pulling down a book. "I don't know the name."

"A repair manual for the soul," Lou answered.

"You're a man of many talents."

"And master of none?"

"I was trying to be nice."

Lou noticed the tension in his stomach. What was he defending? What did he want from April? She had stayed in contact with him despite his busy schedule. And hers.

31

"Does this work?" April asked, pointing to an old wood stove.

"It's the only source of heat."

"Except for people."

Lou moved a large wooden owl and Jennie's math book off a small table, so he could set down a tray. He and April drank tea. She wrapped herself in a wool blanket that was lying on the old couch.

"Yeah, it took us a while and here we are," April said.

"If you stay long enough, you can see the rest of the house."

"Is that an invitation or a threat?"

Lou liked the way the edges of her mouth curled in a smile. He sipped his tea.

"All these carvings are of wild animals," she observed, looking around the room. "Do you like any tamed ones?"

"Such as?"

"Me." April moved a little closer to him on the couch. "Your hackles didn't rise did they?"

"I'm not sure I have hackles."

"I want to check."

She leaned closer and touched the back of his neck. Lou sat motionless.

"Damn, this is hard for me, Lou." She pulled her hand away.

Lou leaned forward and blew on his tea.

"April, you're smart and pretty. I like talking to you."

"So, why are we moving so slowly?"

"Kids, work, my age, history. To me, we're on a fast-moving train and there's a tunnel straight ahead."

"Is that a sexual image?"

"Jennie's spending the night at a friend's."

April flushed. "Yarrow is spending the night at a friend's."

"I don't want you to make all the moves."

"'Something is happening here,' as that old song goes."

"An experiment."

"That's a little cold."

Lou leaned over and kissed her. She kissed back.

"That was a little warmer." April looked at him. "Hey, maybe you could show me the rest of your house."

"That won't take long."

Lou and April went out onto his little deck. The slight wind pushed the tree branches around and made a subtle rustling song.

"Careful by the railing," Lou said.

"It's so quiet," April said. "Not like my apartment."

"My writer friend said, 'There's beautiful music inside my head.' I think of that when I'm here. The wind in the creeks makes its own soft song."

"Lots of space between the notes."

"That's how I like it."

April followed Lou as he walked along the deck. A half-moon had risen in the east over the trees and it filled the evening with a soft grey light.

"Shit, what's that?" April asked. She jumped and grabbed Lou's arm.

"That's my pet coyote," Lou said, laughing. "Don't worry. He's kind of slow."

"Wow, that's a carving."

"It's not alive," he chuckled.

"The way the moonlight hits the grey wood." April bent down and touched it. "Wow. It has a powerful aura around it."

"Aura?"

"You fucking describe it. It's about to spring into the woods."

"His brother's in the bedroom, so don't be spooked."

"You're feeling optimistic." April stood up and gave him a kiss. She looked back at the carving. "Where did you get it?"

"Did you ever see a coyote?" he asked.

"No."

"They live all around here. Once I was up in the forest at dusk by myself. I saw what I thought was a shaggy brown-grey dog. The coyote looked right at me for a while. When I went to sleep that night, I heard it howling. I felt small, with the night and the forest so large, and the coyotes prowling."

A few minutes later, they were sitting on Lou's bed. April disentangled herself from a long kiss and said, "This is our first time. I'm still not sure how this is going to go, so let's be kind, at least."

Three hours later, Lou was walking naked, a little chilly, on the deck. He had slept long enough to have the dream again. He had awakened with a start.

The feeling of April's heat had burrowed deep under his skin, like a sliver, or a second heart. She was close to something core in him. Was it fear, excitement? Could he surrender to that feeling? Did he want to?

In the distance, a coyote howled at the bright half-moon, now high in the sky, illuminating the deck and the surrounding oak trees.

I'm so tired. That damn nightmare, he thought. *Everything is moving so fast. But I have my art to hold on to.*

He leaned his arms on the shaky railing and looked out into the forest.

Chapter 9

The Heart of Grief

"Thanks for visiting, Lou," Casey said. "She's sleeping now."

"How is she?"

Casey's deck duplicated Lou's, overlooking the dry creek bed. The two men sat together on old beach chairs.

"All seemed fine, then this damn infection. This woman came to help us. The first thing she says to me, 'I see the pain in your eyes.' We were sitting right here."

"Who is she?"

"Hospice."

"Hospice? Wow. That was quick."

"No shit. This woman asks, 'Is she near the end, la termina?' I had just gotten back from my walk and I said, 'It's so hard to leave her.' All of a sudden, I'm talking to her like she's my best friend."

"Everything has happened so fast."

"Then I said to this woman, 'Her smaller and smaller circle of perambulation...' I was talking in circles, not making a lot of sense. I am so tired. So I waved my hand up there, towards the hills, and said, 'She knows all the wildflowers.'"

"She says, 'Si, senor. I am sorry for you. You carry so much love for her. Where are your sons?' That shut me up. I wish those goddamn kids... Lou, I don't know when she will stop breathing. They sent her home to die. How could this happen? She says she doesn't want to leave me."

"Of course."

Casey studied the little fenced-in garden in front of the porch, then said, "I just can't keep up with everything. She loves the roses, but I never learned how to tend them. She looks at me, while she's lying in bed. It was like she's my whole life, everything that matters. The loss I am about to feel opens up in me like a canyon in my stomach. I almost felt sick. I know this doesn't make any sense."

Lou heard the clatter of rocks falling into the creek and said, "You make me want to love someone that much."

Casey looked out into the forest. "Are you sure? You can't get ready for this part."

"Doctors don't know everything."

"Look in on her before you go."

"I will." For a moment, Lou heard the wind whispering through the redwoods. It didn't calm him down, as it usually did. He remembered Jennie running after his truck when he had to leave the farm. The look on her face.

"I felt something like that, once. You can't get ready. It just happens."

Casey continued, "I said to the helper woman, her name is Angela, 'She will take the longest trip of all, the finito. I said things to her that I regret.' Lou, why am I telling you all this?"

Lou looked at his friend and sipped his beer. "It's okay."

"Angela says, 'You can say her forgiveness you.' I almost laughed when I heard her fractured English. She says, 'Senor. You tell to me all."

"So I said, to her, 'Before she fell, we had some hard times. The kids were in college. She seemed mad all the time, and I didn't know why. I was coming to the end of my work. No mas trabador? I wasn't sure what I would do then. I imagined some cruises, a trip to Greece maybe. Women teachers came on to me. But I couldn't do it to her.' I don't think Angela understood..."

"Maybe she did."

"She sat still as a statue. I felt warmth coming off her, her care." Casey took a sip of beer. "Lou, love is going to break you, no matter what you choose to do. Angela says, after a while, 'It is hard for you, no?' I snapped, 'Hard. You don't know hard.' Then she told me a story about her life and I felt embarrassed that I'd snapped at her."

"We all get stupido," Lou said, and they clinked glasses. "Go on."

"Angela says, 'Mi hijo, the army picked him up, for nada. Mi esposo went to look for him at the jail of the government and he never came back. Both of them gone. I walked four days to the border. I thought they would look for me.'"

"That shut me up. I went to a talk about caretaker burnout. I got so mad. Rules to take care of yourself. What are you going to do, go on a vacation when your spouse is dying? I wish I could keep up with the goddamned roses." He put his head in his hands.

Lou looked at the grey-green rocks in the creek bed.

"If I give in to the tears, I'll never stop crying. And she still looks out for me. She said last week, 'Oh, when I am gone, you can start dating and find someone who's healthy, whom you can have sex with.' I don't know what she is thinking. Death is going to rip my heart out. Bad knees, no hair, bad shoulder. Some prize. Does this make sense at all?"

"You sound angry," Lou said.

"I'm not mad at you. Not yet." Casey laughed harshly. "You're a good friend. Angela and I were sitting right here, before we had gone in to meet Lily. She walked behind my chair and put her hands on my shoulders. It had been weeks since someone touched me with that kind of kindness. I reached up and felt wetness on my face. I hadn't cried in years.

"Lou, I swear to God, you promise 'in sickness and in health.' You're young. You don't think, it means this. It's so hard. All I want to do is watch her breathe. Then I get tired, I get angry and bored. I want something to happen."

Lou looked up as a small brown bird fluttered by the deck.

"Sometimes I just want her to die," Casey said. "I'm too tired."

Chapter 10

The Fall at the Food Pantry

"I never thought I'd be here," Mrs. Goodwin said to Lou. She pushed her walker past the long table laden with metal bins full of carrots, broccoli, and cauliflower. "I thought the money... Never mind." She made a dismissive gesture with her free hand.

Lou looked down the long line of Bingo residents filling boxes and bags with free food. One couple wore REI clothing more expensive than his jeans and sweatshirt. A long-haired young man had leaves on the back of his sweater from sleeping outside.

"Okay."

"Your plumbing job just barely holds water."

"Welcome to the food pantry, Mrs. Goodwin."

"Don't change the subject. Those politicians take all my money selling democracy. What about my social security? Is someone going to help me out to the car?"

"Did you drive down here?"

"You know I can't. My neighbor..."

"We can find one of the teens to..."

"Don't interrupt. You're too good to help?"

"No, I just..."

"I'll get by." Mrs. Goodwin waved her hand and moved down the line of tables, towards stacks of egg cartons. "Yes, I'll get by." A cardboard box perched precariously on the narrow seat of her walker.

Lou said hello to a young blond mother with a shoeless three-year-old in tow.

"Yo, lots of fresh veggies today," Laura, one of the volunteers, said to Lou.

"Yeah, but none of it's organic," said Jessie, a heavy-set, mid-twenties man who came every week.

"It's free," Lou said.

"You can eat chemicals," Jessie said. "I'd rather be hungry."

After Jessie limped down the line, Laura smiled and said, "Fussy vegan assholes."

"A new class: the entitled poor." Lou laughed.

"He could use a few days without food."

The hall filled with bustling Hispanic families, more elders with walkers, a young tattooed twenty-something, and a grey-haired hippy with a camo-colored backpack slung over his shoulder.

Food bank volunteers replenished the long tables that filled the community hall with cans of vegetables, out-of-date bread, apples, plums, carrots, and spaghetti from boxes kept behind the display tables.

"It's our own little grocery store." Reverend Jones stood next to Lou, after he had walked through the hall, hugging people.

"I'm glad you started it," Lou replied. "I still can't call them 'customers'."

"Can you think of a better term?"

"My brothers and sisters, after Jesus?" Lou said.

The minister laughed. "You are quick, Lou. But sadly, Jesus never said 'sisters'. Thanks for coming down."

A black woman came over and gave the Reverend a hug.

"Morning, Sarah," the reverend said, "How's it going?"

"It's going, reverend. Thanks for being here." She moved down the line, rolling a small metal cart.

Lou wandered through the hall, saying hello to people. He picked up a few onions which had escaped from someone's bag.

Suddenly the sounds of a crash filled the hall. Lou ran outside and saw, in the courtyard, three women volunteers crouched around an elderly man who had fallen on the steps. Rev. Jones pushed his way into the circle.

After a quick physical check, Rev. Jones motioned to Lou and another man. "Let's get him up on a chair. I think he is fine."

Lou smelled alcohol. "I've got a first aid kit."

"Ice from the kitchen should do," the reverend said. "Jackie?"

"What?" the elderly man asked, looking around.

Lou returned to the community room. Mrs. Goodwin came down the line, filling her box with day-old bagels.

"Is he going to sue the church?" she asked Lou. "For making him get free food?"

"Ambulance chasers are lining up," Lou responded. He noticed that she looked tired. "Are you okay?"

Mrs. Goodwin carefully sorted through the bread, reading labels. "Sugar, sugar, sugar. Who can eat this... I almost said shit."

"I've heard that word."

"I bet you have. Am I supposed to thank you for your help? All you did was stare at me."

"Nice to see you too, Mrs. Goodwin."

She carefully put two loaves of bread on top of her box and walked towards the door.

Lou picked up a few large waxed vegetable boxes and took them to the recycling dumpster. Back inside, he mopped up a milk spill and said hello to a couple of young Mexican girls, who giggled at him.

There was another crash in the courtyard.

That evening, Lou and Casey sat on Lou's deck, talking about Mrs. Goodwin's fall.

"She lay on her back, surrounded by solicitous volunteers and customers. 'Get back,' she said. 'Where's Lou? I want Lou. Don't touch me.'"

Lou's voice caught in his throat.

"She knows you care about her," Casey said. "Are you okay?"

"Yeah, sure. I mean something to her. But am I going to wind up like her, living alone, in the precarious future? Jennie gone somewhere."

"Are you wondering if your carvings will keep you warm?"

"The price of being an artist."

"That's bullshit. You're too young to worry about aging alone."

Lou laughed. "What should I worry about?"

"April's biological clock."

"You think she wants to have a kid with me?"

41

"She's not going to wait for you forever."

"She just started." Lou laughed. "Give her time."

"That's not funny. It's weird. I guess. Time recycles itself. I may be on the verge of letting Lily go, and you're starting..."

"What?"

"How should I know? I've got to get back to Lily, Lou. Good night."

Chapter 11

Dr. Shrank Rattles On

*N*ice house, Lou thought as he walked up the long curve of brick steps.

Dr. Shrank let Lou in the tall oak double doors. "Do you want coffee?"

"A quick one. Miles to go."

"Nice. Frost, you know. He was a real psycho. Wrote all the time. He used pen and paper. I'm writing a book with my iPad. It's stored in the cloud. I'm going intergalactic. Here, try this espresso. I've got a one-of-a-kind four-thousand-dollar Italian... You don't care. Let's go out on the deck."

Dr. Shrank walked Lou through a high-ceilinged living room, and out onto a large redwood deck.

"Maybe I drank too much coffee out here. Wore out the joints or planks, whatever. It was my girlfriend's fault. She fell through that hole.

"You know, Freud was an M. Fucking D. Just like me. I went to UCLA. Now every woman with a crystal and a feather in Bingo calls herself a psychotherapist. Twelve years in medical school and I'm competing with ex-massage therapists.

"That's why it's taken me two years to get the money for the deck. Watch out for that other hole. How's the coffee? Great, I'm sure. How's your business? Let's sit here."

Dr. Shrank sat down on the steps leading up to another deck.

"I'm getting by," Lou said. "Lots of jobs like this. Wood wears out." He looked around at tens of thousands of dollars in repairs. The redwood forest was so damp, it softened the wood.

"I know. I know. It'll be expensive. I don't want to know. When I finish my book, the repair will seem like chump change. I'll be famous. More coffee? I should mainline this shit. It calms me down. I can feel it. And Lou, you calm me down, too. I know you won't burn me, rip me off. So many chiselers and scam artists out there."

"Thanks," Lou said. Dr. Shrank's tremors and rapid speech made him nervous.

"You are a restless tool of low-wage capitalism, a representative of the underground economy, rootless. I don't mean to offend you. Insecure attachments. I see you watching the time. Traumas in your past I could weep for, but don't really want to hear about."

"A restless tool?" Lou interrupted. "I'm here to repair your deck. You're not my fucking doctor."

"Okay, you hate your father. It's not my fault."

Lou waved his hand at the three-story house and the landscaping. "You want all this shit, Doctor. I don't. I'm surfing the waves of capitalism. Finding time for love and art."

"Strange. You don't look like an optimist. Whatever. I thought you could take the truth. I'm empathetic as hell when I'm on the clock. Right? With my patients. You gotta pay to play. Know what I mean? You don't do woodworking at home, do you? You probably go hunting with a bow and arrow."

"Ah, I actually do woodworking at home." Lou kept contradicting Dr. Shrank's proclamations. Why did he care?

"I'm a spiritual teacher. A psychiatrist would want to listen to you talk about your identity crisis. You're having a big one. I can tell by the edge in your voice. Freud and Jung, and all their sycophantic followers through the decades, they already tried listening. Look around you. Has it worked? Is the world a better place? What a waste."

"I never tried psychotherapy."

"I can tell. Oh, trust me, I can tell. I believe in the 'strong man' theory of psychiatry. I force-feed my patients information until I heal them, until they grow up. I read manuals on interrogation by U.S. Special Forces instructors. They know how to get shit done."

"Great," Lou said. "You can get a job interrogating Muslims."

"Well, that's more fun than asking Americans how they feel. Bunch of losers. Once I get my book out, I'll be famous. I don't really want fame. No. Oh, okay, I want to be known all around the world, but is that fame? I don't know. The working title: *Listen to Me*. Isn't that great? No, I don't want any feedback from you."

"I understand."

"No, you don't. A person like you could never understand me."

"Doctor, can we talk a little more about the job?"

"Sure, in a minute. Lou, you and I, we're alike. Everyone needs us. If they only knew it. Bunch of losers. You and I, we watch people from a distance, a safe, loving, respectful distance. We have our mental commentaries. Silent, brilliant observers."

"I'm like you?"

"Except for med school."

"And reading torture manuals."

"Don't be so holier than thou. You eat meat, don't you? Listen, if people want my opinions, they can ask. But until then, I'm content to just be. To 'be' in the fullest, most beautiful Zen sense of the word. The primordial stillness. The Alan Watts peace zone. To just be. I have a lot more to say about this stillness. Just give me a minute while I make some more coffee. You're good?"

Lou sat on the worn deck, not moving. Deck boards and railings sagged everywhere. Except for the cost of Jennie's food, clothes, clubs and school books, he'd tell Dr. Shrank 'thanks but no thanks.' *So this is what parenting feels like*, he thought. There was no place he could send Jennie back to.

He exhaled. Rain the night before had filled the creek behind Dr. Shrank's house. The sound of water always settled him. Little rivulets ran through the redwood forest and across many rocks. Carefully built stone walls had sculpted the hillside into little beds for rhododendrons and camellias.

But the rock walls were cracking under the weight of the slowly eroding earth. Leaves from the overhanging oak trees had started to bury the landscaping. To Lou, the whole forested landscape, including the beautiful shiny-leaved bushes, the sculpted beds, and the deck, was heading into the creek in a calm, unstoppable slide, accompanied by the music of the creek.

Doctor Shrank returned with two porcelain espresso cups on a silver tray, with a silver sugar bowl and a cream pitcher. He put the tray down and sat nearby. He took a deep breath and exhaled.

"Looking through the window, I saw you, Lou. Just sitting. Waiting for something to happen. I admired your quiet. I felt myself relax. I get nervous when people are in my house. I don't know why. Of course, the meds I just took help a lot."

The doctor's hands had quit trembling.

"You and I are alike, Lou. Did I say that already? Meditative, sensitive observers of life in all its awful beauty and tragedy. I feel the mix of your stillness and your anxiety. Sitting with you is like counter punching a skilled boxer."

Lou sipped his coffee.

"The answer to your quest is right here. Bingo. All places look different when you're running. When you're still, everywhere is unique, beautiful, the same. Like my yard. I sat out here so many times, when I could have been working. Or writing my book. Or trying to replace the wife who ran off with the tennis instructor.

"I'm conducting an experiment in entropy. What happens if I do nothing? Yes, I watch the rocks across the creek fall down. I watch the rain slowly destroy my deck. I plant rhododendrons. I do nothing and everything. At the same time. It's the Dao. Like why it's time to fix the deck now. I can't afford another girlfriend falling through it."

Lou's work always brought him in contact with people. Their desires. Their loneliness. He could feel Dr. Shrank's desperate need to connect and his inability to do so. *Do people feel like this around me?* he thought.

He finished his espresso in one gulp. He said, "I'll work for you, Dr. Shrank. But I won't be your patient, your friend, or your student."

Dr. Shrank's eyes got wide. Lou thought, *he is listening.*

Chapter 12

Jennie Surprises April at School

"Remember when we were at the beach and you told me that you didn't know how to be a parent?" April asked.

"Of course," Lou said. They were grabbing a quick dinner at Sushi Central after work.

"I told Jennie I wouldn't tell you, but I need to."

"You look worried."

"I think it's the wasabi that went up my nose." April smiled and looked around the vegan sushi restaurant. "All this chrome and metal makes me feel cold."

"Okay."

"I like my job, you know. It's like being an older friend to girls who are struggling with self-esteem and body issues."

"Jennie came to see you?"

"She did. There are two other counselors. I told her right away that it wasn't a good idea." April hesitated. "She says, 'April, I know you don't like me.' I said, 'I'm dating your father.' She says, 'Are you?' Believe me, I wasn't ready for that conversation."

Lou had stopped eating. "I can see why." Where was April going with this?

"Jennie starts right in and says, 'I dreamt I was running fast through a strange town. People were staring at me. Then someone touched my face and I slowed down, got very calm. All today, I'm so jumpy, teary. What should I do? I don't want your advice.' Then she sat up straighter. 'Today, I can't hold any food down. I'm throwing up all the time.'"

"Shit," Lou said.

"Try to remember that half of my job takes place in the theater of the absurd. I have no idea if kids are making stuff up…"

"Well, is she?"

"Hold on. It's a story. Jennie says, 'I'm fat. One of the boys said so. Sometimes I cut myself, to stop from throwing up.' She turns in her chair and shows me a wide red stain on her torn jeans. I lean over and touch her leg. 'It looks like pizza,' I say. 'Is that a piece of pepperoni?'"

"Well, did she cut herself?"

"Hold on. Then she says, 'Now I can report you for touching me. You'll have to leave town.'"

"Wow," Lou said. "She got it all going."

"That's right. She tells me the dream, now she has to distract me. Actually, she did a pretty good job of upsetting me. I said, 'You're going to run me out of town with a pizza stain and some bullshit story? I don't think so. I live here, Jennie. You'll be gone before I will.'

"Jennie looks at me and says, 'Did my dad tell you something?' You know my office, photos of girls clubs and cheerleaders."

"Right."

"So Jennie looks around and says, 'I hate this town. Look at these beige walls. You don't put up pictures of tats, purple hair, boys with zits. Conform, conform, that's all this school wants. All you want. This is me, bitch. Take it or leave it.'"

April drank her Japanese beer and said, "Then she says, 'I'm pretty sure we're leaving. And you're not coming with us.' When she said that, I felt my heart lurch."

Lou reached across his plate and took her hand.

"Then she says, 'I hate you. Stay away from my father.' And she runs out of the office. I follow her to the back of the school and she sits down in the bleachers. Coaches were putting the boys through football practice.

"Yarrow joined Jennie on the wooden benches. I don't know how he knew where she was. I climbed the stairs and sat a few rows behind them. Awkward. I wanted to make sure Jennie was all right. Jennie looked at Yarrow and said in a soft voice, 'I wanted to tell her. It was Mom in the dream. She used to read to me, and when she finished, she would put her face right in front of me and pat my face with her hands. I wish she could pat my face one more time, like that. One more time.'

"Then she fell silent. She put her head down. Her long hair covered her face. I watched the boys running sprints. I felt for

Jennie, so much, and I started to cry. Yarrow noticed me. He put his arm around Jennie and said, 'We're fine now.' So I left."

"Wow, quite a visit," Lou said.

"When we get this caught up in each other's shit, it's almost like we're a family."

"Almost." And Lou thought, *almost.*

Chapter 13

Jennie Meets Lou's Rat at the Wrong Time

"**D**ad, there's a rat under my bed," Jennie screamed. The sound reverberated in the small cabin. April and Lou were sitting outside, watching leaves fall across the creek bed, as the sun set through the redwoods. Jennie ran out on the deck.

Lou laughed. "It's not just any rat. It's endangered. I'm doing a whole series."

"You'll be endangered if you keep..."

"What?" April said.

"He puts these carvings all around the house, to scare me."

"No, I don't."

Jennie was trembling. "You know I was nervous about April coming for dinner, and now..."

"I put it there a week ago."

"You are a shitty father. You're a good artist, but a shitty father."

"How did I know you'd find it now?"

"Is that how you apologize?" Jennie turned to April. "I'm trying to make a good first impression here. Well, third impression, I guess, counting ... Let's just pretend that didn't happen, you know, at school."

"Okay," April agreed. Jennie sat down on a battered wicker chair on the deck.

"I want all of my dad's attention. When you're here, I get nervous. Like, does he like you more? It shows how fucked up I feel. Excuse my French."

Jennie started to cry and to wave her hand in front of her face.

"Ah," Lou said, looking at April.

"Ah," she said. "She's your kid, Lou."

Jennie said. "Could you two get over yourselves and hand me a fucking Kleenex? I'm fine. I'll do homework. I hope this damn chair doesn't break. That would really make my day. I hate our furniture."

"No, come with us," April said. "We'll get tacos in town."

Rain had fallen that afternoon, and Lou, Jennie and April walked through fall oak and maple leaves on the way to town. A cold wind blew in from the north. Lou didn't know whom to put his arm around, so he took both of their hands and walked between them.

While Lou and April lingered over dessert, Jennie went off to meet some friends who were skateboarding on the Parkade, a raised parking area in the middle of downtown.

"I saw the bald eagle on the mantle."

"It's a little hard to miss."

"And the owl landing on the stick. Clever."

"Yes."

"You have a gift. But Jennie talks about it more than you do."

"How do you like the pie?"

"You must have tools, a shop."

"Yeah."

"You must have had a teacher. Please don't say 'yeah.'"

"My father. April, look, I make things. People like to look at them. Okay. They all have theories, ideas. I don't know."

"Last question, okay? Do you ever have shows?"

"It wasn't much fun, the gallery thing."

"Gallery? Where did you…?"

"I love peach pie when it's in season, don't you?"

"Okay, okay. I'm going home tonight. That's pretty obvious."

"Well, I asked Jennie to sleep in the truck. She refused."

"You did what?"

"Joke. She likes you, though."

"She doesn't make that obvious. But, Lou, we both have these little houses. What are we going to do?"

"About?"

"If I have to spell it out, maybe you don't want it." April put her fork down with a clatter. "Shit. This is the most embarrassing conversation I've had in a while."

Lou moved his plate out of the way and touched April's hand. "Sometimes you want us to move forward, then sometimes you don't."

"It's true. I'm confused too. I'm too old to be confused."

"Once I get my stuff in the truck, I don't know where I'll

unpack it."

"What does that mean?" April asked. She pulled back and looked. "Fuck your 'rambling-man' bullshit, Lou. My life is not a country-and western song. And fuck my 'co-dependent, can't-live-without-you' bullshit. Those were the old days."

"Okay."

"And you have Jennie. You can't just wander off and pull her out of school."

"Who says? Her stuff will fit in the truck."

"How can you be that self-centered?"

"You're right." He reached towards her. "I like you. I don't want to move away."

"Sha-na-na-na, live for today." April quoted an old song. "Yarrow and I can't live like that. Or Jennie. You can't just break this up on a whim."

"Whim?"

"Okay. Wrong word."

Chapter 14

At the Alibi

"At the bike bar next door, apparently they've outlined motorcycles," Pete said.

"Outlawed, I think you mean," Lou said. After five beers, Pete wasn't making much sense. Lou was relaxing at the Alibi, the local's local bar. "You've had a few." Pete's company was fine, early in the evening.

"You worked late." Pete laughed. "Not me."

"Plumbing." Lou sipped his beer, glad Friday had come.

"Enough said," Pete replied. He, too, worked as a contractor/handyman. "Next door at The Trans-Mission, you know, populated by assholes from somewhere else with their six-thousand-dollar bikes." Pete's anger grew the more he drank.

The after-work buzz of friends filled the old bar, with its 49er banners and pictures of local sports heroes fading on the walls.

"Last week I was sitting over there," Pete continued.

"You went next door. Why?"

"Rich chicks."

"You'll need a Polartec jacket, dude, not that." Lou gestured with his beer at Pete's torn Levi's vest.

"What's Polartec? I was figuring out what beer to order. List had, like, fifty beers on it and I never heard of any of them. Someone rams one of these expensive bikes into my back. Then says, 'Excuse me,' like I shouldn't be sitting in his bar. I jumped up, but I couldn't get to him because of all the bikes coming in. All those fag spandex outfits, too."

"I wondered why you were really there." Lou laughed.

"Head-to-toe condoms," Pete said.

Lou laughed so hard, he spat up a little beer.

"The Alibi works for me," Pete continued. "Lou, my friend, you aren't one of those rich assholes from somewhere else. You're just an asshole from somewhere else."

Lou smiled. "Thanks, Pete. Good to know I belong. If I close my eyes, this place smells looks like Eureka." He looked up at the row of beer bottles in front of the long mirror above the bar. He recognized many of the names from ads on Super Bowl Sunday.

Pete called hello to friends coming and going. Nursing his beer, Lou started to get that familiar I'm-a-stranger-here feeling. He wondered, what are all these people talking about? He didn't understand what was interesting to them.

"Whoa, man, long time no see." Pete jumped out of his chair and gave someone a bear hug. "Come and join us. Shit, you're all wet."

"What did you expect? It's raining." When the man came around a post, Lou saw that Johnie, his landlord, had arrived. "Louie, Louie, move over," Johnie said. He had never called Lou that before. Johnie swerved when he sat down, then he placed his beer carefully on the table near Pete's empties. "Louie works for me now."

"I know that, Johnie. It's been two years," Pete said. "God help you, Lou."

"Hey, let the past rest."

"I'm a contractor now, not some day laborer for the massa. Social immobility, right?"

"That's social mobility," Lou corrected.

"Pete and I went to high school together."

Pete continued his dark monologue. "Your dad, that cheap fuck, said my dad..."

Johnie interrupted. "Last time we went over this bullshit, we were sitting over there at that table. You said everything worked out. I'll get another round. Fucking chill out by the time I get back."

"Yes, boss," Pete said, tilting back another beer.

The alcohol buzz of humor was getting louder, encompassing the twenty or so men in the bar, their histories, the stories they were telling. Lou felt their comradeship, a way they cared about each other, as they tried to outdo each other with stories of work, drinking and sex.

But he had arrived in Bingo only a few years ago. He couldn't argue about his father's hassles, like Pete and Johnie, or about the increase in county property taxes. His heart felt a little hollow.

The bar looked like a hundred bars he'd been in: neon glowing beer advertisements, battered chairs and tables, liquor bottles in rows behind the bar itself. A lingering smell of beer, piss and some cigarette smoke, drifting in from the back patio. A game on the television, but no one watched it.

He thought of Eureka again. *Why couldn't he just stay where he was born? Well, that was obvious.*

Johnie's round face looked redder and redder, as he pounded down beer after beer. Lou and Pete had quit trying to keep up with him. Lou was looking for an exit line.

"Remember we used to climb up in the trees and throw apples at the wetbacks who came to tend the apple trees?" Johnie asked.

"When you hit one guy, you laughed so hard that your mother heard us."

"God rest her soul."

Lou tuned out. Now the background hum of the bar soothed him. He had money for food, for beer. He had work for the next week or two. He belonged.

Then Johnie raised his voice. "No, no. Pete, you don't know anything. You never did. We were sitting in this bar. Dad and I. He said, 'We can't afford Frank and his family anymore.' I knew you had to leave.' 'Where will Pete go?' I asked. I was about twelve."

"No, man, no. Water under the dam…" Pete's voice trailed off.

"I wanted you and your family to stay. But Dad said, 'This is your legacy, my name and my farm. Don't let go of it.' And I was grateful. I thought, this is my father's gift. Two years after he died, I figured out my father had mortgaged everything so he could gamble. Selfish prick."

"You'll figure it out," Pete said. "You'll keep…" Again, he couldn't finish his thought.

"I'm drowning in debt. Last week, some Mexican fucking hombre walks up my driveway and offers me cash for the whole farm. For a second, just a second, I thought, this sounds good. Then I looked around at the orchard and at the tombstones out behind the house. I remembered what my father said."

"You forgot how he fucked you," Pete added.

Johnie shot him a look, then paused, as if he had forgotten the topic.

"What did you say?" Pete reminded him.

"Fuck, no. I yelled at Senor fucking Jose to get off my property."

National news broke into the sports talk on the TV suspended over the bar. "Dark-skinned man wounds three at Christian church in Alabama. Terrorist attack."

The bartender turned up the volume, and many faces turned towards the news. Johnie continued. "And the fucking fence hopper says, 'Okay, amigo. Maybe I'll come back, when you're more desperate.' I'm not desperate and I'm not his amigo. And this is what I'm talking about. Immigrants want to take over. California is white."

Pete shook his head. "I never heard this shit until after Maria dumped you."

"Fuck her and all her kids. It's all going out of control," Johnie mumbled. He was looking down at his glass of beer. "The border is a sieve, and no one is protecting us. Drug dealing beaners want to buy up all the land in Bingo. Spics buying me out. It ain't right."

"You tell him, Johnie," a drunk in a flannel shirt yelled from the next table. "You tell him. Wetbacks are taking over baseball, too."

His buddy at the table yelled, "Taking over dope growing..."

"No one wants your property," Lou said. "The whole place is a tear-down."

"Shut up, Lou. That's your fault. You're just another migrant laborer. Only you're white. And sometimes I doubt that. You're so fucking lazy."

"What did you say?" Lou said. He stood up and began picking up his change off the table

"When the spics start voting, they'll do to us what we did to them in the Bear Republic. Take all the land. Kill all of us. History is..." Johnie ran out of steam and sat down hard in his chair. He finished off another beer.

"Johnie, come on, I'll walk you home," Pete said.

"No," Johnie shouted. He stood up and brushed beer glasses and bottles off the table with a quick sweep of his hand. "No. No one is listening to me."

"That's right, you prick," Lou said as he turned towards the door.

Chapter 15

A Death in the Family

"I've got to tell someone," Casey said. "I'm coming apart."
"That's normal," Lou said. Sitting together on Casey's deck, the two men were bundled up against the damp fall air.

"You think so now."

The sound of the season's rain running down through the creek bed soothed Lou. He had liked Lily, and her death had rocked the Orchard community.

"The first night after she died, I slept so hard, it's like I brought the whole town to a standstill. Last night I couldn't sleep at all. Only dream; of chasing some wild animals, of being chased, of small babies who cannot be saved in their hospital beds. I woke up to pee, couldn't get back to sleep." Casey paused and looked at Lou.

"I don't know what to say. Can I make you some tea?"

"It's my house. Just sit there and listen. I had this weird caregiver at the end. Last week, she put her hands on my shoulders and massaged them. I couldn't remember the last time... That night, I dreamed an awful sexy dream of a large, dark woman who pursued me in a great, dark castle. Then I pursued her while she ran through bedroom after bedroom. Finally, I leapt on her and sank into her big arms."

Lou said, "A dream doesn't make you a bad person. It's cold out here. Are you okay?"

"I'm burning. Like a fever. It's so wild to be telling you all this. Where did Lily go? Where is she?"

"The great question."

"Once this Angela woman arrived from Hospice, I started waking up with a raging hard-on. Like three, four days in a row. Lily's last days. I almost didn't remember what that felt like. Stop me if this is Too Much Information."

"No. It's fine."

"I jump out of bed when the night attendant leaves at six a.m.

Lily always told me, 'No resuscitation.' Okay. So I watch her, breathing, rasping away. Day after day."

Casey paused again and looked up the hill into the redwoods. "Now I know which cars my neighbors drive, when they leave for work. Whose dogs howl. It's like I'm the one who's dying."

"That's so intense," Lou said.

"Laundry, walking to the store. Taking out the trash. I used to command an empire. Not really. But I had a classroom, then an office. I could make things happen. Now, nothing. Powerless."

"Death does that."

"Don't lecture me. See I'm not, really, not so powerless. I could sit there and love my wife. I could breathe for her. Powerlessness says no to life, to Lily. I was never going to say that."

"So you sat there, like a warrior."

"Thanks. Or maybe a fool. When Death came for her, I could do nothing. But that's not what I need to talk about... We moved Lily into the guest bedroom because of the hospital bed and the all-night care. Why was dying so fucking complicated? I always hated the wallpaper in that room.

"On that last morning, I took Lily's hand. I breathed with her and wept for a few minutes, then got up to make my coffee. She woke up later in the morning. With the angle of the bed, and my bad back, getting her upright was hard.

"She ate some soup. Exhaustion filled every bone in my body. She slept and woke up, then she stared blankly at the ceiling. Did she even know I was there? She murmured something. I leaned over the bed. Was she saying, 'Go for it. Go for it'?"

Casey looked out into the forest. "It's so quiet out there. I never dreamed those were her last words."

"You never know."

"I realized it's not the words she said, but the vast silence that would follow and never end. I leaned forward again. Maybe she would say to me, "I always loved you."

Casey stopped there and swallowed a couple of times. "Maybe she would say..." He stopped again.

"She didn't have to say that to you, Casey."

"Okay. Be consoling. She didn't say it. Angela came in the afternoon. She wore a big woven dress and that crazy hat. She swept up the kitchen and living room. Who knew there could be so much laundry? She kept looking at me. I felt like I wanted to fall into her arms, or I wanted her to leave. I was so tired, it was like I was someone else.

"While she was banging around, she said, 'Are your hijos, sons coming?' She spoke so tenderly. Then I realized I was mad at them. Sure they had come and visited. Then paid for a nurse. An act of generosity. An act of abandonment. I wanted Bill and Charlie to be sitting with me on the porch, not Angela.

"Angela took off her big, strange hat and placed it on the table between us. She said, 'Senor, yesterday, I should not touch you. They make the rules I should not.' I took her hand and said, 'No. You are so kind. I needed...'" Casey stopped there.

Lou sat in Casey's wicker chair. The creek noise soothed him. Death, life. It was all happening around him. What was Casey gathering himself to say?

"Then she said, 'I was thinking I could give more today, if you want.' 'I'd have to pay you for a massage.' 'No, senor. My heart to yours.' The way she spoke so softly, I could almost drop into this wave of grief in my heart."

Lou heard the afternoon UPS truck threading its way through the narrow lanes of the Orchard. Kids on the climbing toy whooped and shouted next door.

"We went inside and I lay down on my bed and took off my shirt. She rubbed my back for a while. She said, 'Senor, do not worry now. Just be quiet. What will happen to Mrs. Lily, it will happen.' I felt my body relax, for the first time in months."

"Now, senor, I learned some things in my country. I can try. Tell me if you don't like.' She lay down full length on me. I felt as if she would crush me, or swallow me. This is so embarrassing."

Casey looked away, out into the forest. "Sometimes I just want to walk out into the oaks and redwoods and keep going."

"Okay." Lou felt strange, and also embarrassed. He felt there was something here, a vast experience bigger than Casey's story. Death, loss, comfort.

"She moved very gently and we sank together into the bed. My skin felt this intense hunger to be touched. Totally. Warmly. She said, 'In my country, we believe the skin is a great healer.' I could feel her breath on my ear.

"'Senor, can you roll over on your side? I can massage your chest and face. Here, let me help you get out of your pants. No, don't worry. And por favor tell me if this hurts in any way.' We were spooning. I felt so warm with her behind me.

"She lay down with me, holding me. I felt so young, and I felt the massive warmth of her breasts against my back. 'Do not worry, senor.'"

Lou finally realized where the story was going.

"I was hard as a rock, not easy for a pensioner. She stroked my face and chest. Then she said, 'Let's roll over, senor.' Then she shifted her dress a little and all of a sudden, I was inside her. I didn't know whether to struggle or to relax. The warm, slippery softness felt so good. Like my world had been so dry, so brittle, with Lily so sick and here was all the warmth and softness in the world. I started to weep uncontrollably. Angela said, 'It's all right, senor, we can stop any time. It is bueno.'

"'Go for it,' I murmured, and I pushed myself deeply into her again and again. And never stopped crying. After a few minutes of silence, she said, 'Senor, you have given me a great gift, your love and sorrow. I carry them inside me now.'

"I felt a strange peacefulness. I took off all my clothes to clean myself, then I heard Lily, rasping loudly, so loudly. She tried to talk and I leaned over the hospital bed. Lily opened her eyes. And she breathed out one last, final gasp. Stillness filled the room. Angela came in and brought me a blanket. The room was so warm. The two of us sat quietly there for an hour." Casey fell silent. For a long time, Lou listened to the creek and the subtle wind rubbing the redwoods together.

"It was the end of the road. Forty-three years."

"Are you looking for absolution?" Lou asked.

"I'll probably never tell that story again."

"I don't judge you. When you talk about her, it's the love I feel."

"You can love like that, Lou. If you let yourself."

The wind kept playing in the trees, and the temperature dropped some more. Casey went inside and Lou went home.

Chapter 16

A Silent Day at the Beach

"You look tired."

"Yeah." Lou steered his way through a thick carpet of recently-fallen redwood needles. "Water makes the road slick."

"Were you going to talk now? I know we're going to be quiet when we get there," April said.

"This was your idea. Shit," Lou said, swerving. "These goddamn bikers. Why do they all want to go to Pt. Reyes?"

"Actually, it was Casey's idea. Remember, at the café, before... How is he, by the way?"

"Holding on. I'm just starting to get how much he loved Lily."

Lou drove for a few minutes, eyes intent on the road. Then he said, "Okay. I'll tell you a dream, but don't tell me what it means."

"It's my day off."

Lou looked across at her.

"Joke, okay?" She looked down at the creek in a canyon below the road. "The creek is beautiful. I came up here a few times as a kid with my family. I loved it."

"Same theme as ever. My father is pounding his fist on a big table and yelling at me, 'You have to go. You have to stay. You have to go.' He follows me out to my truck, which is loaded with all I own. He throws his cigarette into the back of the truck and it bursts into flame. Then I wake up."

"Your father? You don't talk about him much."

"He's always huge, like King Kong. Afterwards, I couldn't sleep and went out on my deck. Then the sun came up and here I am. I'm so tired. Shit, there's another one. Why don't they ride single file?"

April looked down at the creek through the redwoods again and said, "More than one hundred major schools of dream

65

interpretation could tell you about King Kong."

"What a bunch of shit. Do people always know why they dream certain things?"

"No." She laughed. "How often do you have that dream?"

"Every night."

"No wonder you are always tired."

"Sometimes I just want to get in my truck and drive. Beyond those trees and creeks. What's out there?" Lou got excited and waved his arm at the vast redwood forest.

"You want to drive away from your dream?"

The truck swerved a little. "How the hell should I know? It's not just a commitment issue."

"Slow down, big guy. I want to live long enough to hear about your genuine American wanderlust."

"I sense some sarcasm." Lou smiled.

"I think it's irony. What do those Clint Eastwood types commit to?"

Lou noticed the edge in April's voice. He reached across the truck to take her hand. "Someone like you."

"You don't say much, but it has an impact." April put her other hand over his.

"Sometimes you don't need words," Lou said.

She pulled her hands back and sighed.

The road opened up, past the redwoods, into some rolling grasslands. Lou accelerated past two more bike riders. Some papers attached to a clipboard slid off his dashboard.

"Do you need those?" April asked.

"As long as they stay in the truck." Lou was quiet, focused on driving.

"Okay, try this," Lou said. "The figure of King Kong isn't my father at all. It's really Jennie. Every day she changes her mind about school, friends, does she want to stay, does she like pizza."

"Jennie is King Kong? I think you're messing with me and my whole profession. But I can't talk about it. I'm pledged to silence and awareness."

"Right."

"You don't talk about your father much."

"You said that already." *Am I angry now?* Lou thought. "I don't like therapy. This happens because of that. How does anyone know?"

"Whatever," April said. She returned to looking out the window.

After they parked the truck, they walked over a little hill towards the beach. Oak and bay trees lined the worn path. The soft ground absorbed their footsteps. At the top of the hill, the trees opened up. They could see a wall of light reflecting in the bay.

"Wow, the air is so clear," April said.

"Okay, here we are," Lou said. "All day. No texting. No parenting. No talking. Lying on the beach. Watching the pelicans."

"Not talking about what?"

"There you go." Lou smiled, put down his backpack and spread out his towel. The sun had warmed the sand, although the air was cool. A family with two teen girls was picnicking down the beach.

April had brought a beach chair. A sun hat. A down vest. She sat down, then took a water bottle and a bottle of sunscreen out of her bag.

"Are you settled yet?" Lou asked from under his Giants cap.

"I didn't say a word. Do you ever miss your ex-wife?"

Lou adjusted his hat to keep the sun out and thought for a while. "Not her specifically. But yes, when we were building a life on the land, with Jennie. Hush now."

A soft wind coming up the bay blew the tide up into a little lagoon. It overwhelmed the battlements of a forgotten sandcastle. April took out her phone and put it away.

"It's hard to let go," she said. She watched the cloud formations. "Yarrow is a good boy. His dad can probably take care of him for a whole day. Why did I still hate him so much?"

Lou said nothing.

April smiled. The water washed away a large heart that the two teens had drawn on the beach. A sharp squeal came from an osprey overhead.

"Okay, my problem teens can talk to their parents, or not. Can get pregnant or get tattoos, or not. I can't control them all."

"Not from here."

"Okay, I'm perfectly quiet now."

Lou snorted. A few minutes later, he went for a swim, then toweled himself off and lay down again. The other family gathered up their gear and left. The sun finally moved behind a wall of fog to the west of the beach.

In the truck, April said, "That wasn't so bad. I can see why you like it."

"Okay." Lou turned his truck around in the cul-de-sac and drove out to the main road.

Lou had felt peaceful the whole day. He had enjoyed April more than he thought he would. He knew that he tried to dose his own loneliness with nature. With his artwork. But somehow it was always there. What would satisfy it? April?

"It's hard to think straight when I'm so tired. Sometimes I feel superior to Bingo's residents," he said. "They're so close to this, to the ocean and the beach, but they're in such a rush."

"Your country boy shit again," April interrupted. "People like me. Is that what you're saying? Go fuck yourself... Shit." She stopped talking.

Lou was getting heated, too. "I want to create something new in my dull life, to inspire me, to inspire my artwork. I want to feel alive."

"I'll saddle up your horse, senor. Adios." April looked out the window.

Lou couldn't tolerate her disappointment. "No, listen, April. Sometimes when we're talking, or even like today at the beach, I think my big adventure isn't a place, but you. Adventure and mystery is you." He took her hand again.

"So, I'm like some undiscovered country, like Wyoming? Is that it?" April played with him.

He could see her relaxing, and he did as well. "Maybe more like Idaho."

Chapter 17

Lou Finds Out More About
Johnie Than He Wanted to Know

"Hey, Lou, are you home?" Johnie knocked on the door of Lou's cabin.

Lou looked at him through the battered screen. "What?"

"I was a shit the other day. I know."

"Three weeks ago."

"Really?" Johnie swerved a little and grabbed the railing. "Shit, that's loose too."

"What's in the bag?"

"Tacos and beers."

"I'm making dinner already."

"Open the door, man. I'm trying to apologize."

Lou and Johnie went out on the deck. A little fawn and her mother scampered away, into the thick stand of redwoods.

"I remember trying to shoo those fuckin' deer out of my parents' garden. Never worked." Johnie took containers, beers, forks and napkins out of his bag and spread them around the table. He knocked a Styrofoam container onto the deck, but it didn't open.

"Lucky me, lucky fuckin' me," he said. "Where's your kid?"

"At school."

"All I did there was pound beers and try to get laid."

Two beers were already missing from the six-pack. Lou readied himself for one of Johnie's rants. *Why did I let him in?* he thought.

"I hate this place," Johnie said through a mouthful of taco. "The rundown buildings, the old apple trees. Worrying about fire. Then months of dreary rain, grey days. I'm fucking trapped. Everyone expects me to say how lucky I am. My father's business. What a genius he was. You're the lucky one, Lou. You don't have any roots."

"You don't know me."

"Okay. But you can pack your tools in the truck and go. Oh, shit." Johnie knocked over a salsa container and it splashed on Lou's hand-carved coyote. Lou quickly wiped up the stain.

"No worries, jefe."

"I'm not your fucking 'jefe.'" Johnie gulped down his beer. "Maybe that didn't come out right. My mother, brothers. They tell me to love the Orchard. It's their version of heaven on Earth. They all left."

Johnie stopped drinking for a moment and looked around. "My father. Everyone thinks it's my fault the businesses failed. I drive you like a dog. My life is like a hamster cage that gets smaller every year. I have to yell at someone."

Lou remembered what a prick Johnie had been to him. Was Johnie apologizing, or wasting his time?

"Half my shit is still in boxes, Johnie, and my truck is full of gas. Do you think I care about your crappy cabins?"

"I know you're pissed. But for me, it's worse. You've started over. Bingo is all I know. People I've known all my life. I know what they think."

"You've made your life, amigo," Lou said.

"Just like you, asshole," Johnie said. "Just like you." He raised his can, but Lou didn't clink with him.

"How do you make friends?"

"What?"

"Somewhere new?"

Lou rolled up his brown paper taco wrapper and said, "It's time for me to go and pick up Jennie. She's at play practice."

"Boy, this beer tastes good. At the end of every month, I'm calculating, how much rent came in, who's leaving and how much I owe." Johnie sat slumped over in his chair.

Lou stood up and said, "Give me thirty days notice' when you close."

"Just like that," Johnie said. "You kick me out of my own cabin."

Now the mottled fawn came down out of the forest and into the wet creek bed. The mother hung back, watching the men on the porch. A cool wind blew across the property.

The sky had darkened, from blue to purple to black. The first stars had come up, and the air smelled of earth and pine. The view caught Lou's eye and he lingered for a moment.

"I was born about a hundred yards from here," Johnie said. "Sometimes I love this land. The land, not this goddamned business. I see three generations of gravestones out in the back when I do the dishes. I don't know how to leave that. To become a renter, wandering from town to town. It scares me."

Lou liked the Orchard. To him, it was not full of history and failed dreams. Old, bent fruit trees held their own against time.

"Johnie, I gotta go." He walked towards the deck steps.

"No thanks for dinner. Kicking me out. My own property." Johnie held tight to the loose handrail as he stumbled down the steps. "Gotta get that fixed. Yeah." His speech was coming out very slurred now. Lou turned to him.

"Johnie?"

"Wha.."

"You never got to the apology."

"Fuck you."

Chapter 18

The Mysterious Caregiver

"You look like shit, man," Lou said. He set his coffee down on Casey's table. The coffee shop filled with workers grabbing their morning caffeine.

"What grief looks like," Casey said. He stared at his teacup. "You don't know. This place is so loud. I almost can't stand it. People here are so nosy." He looked at Lou.

"I can go sit somewhere else."

"I'm not mad at you. At myself. She liked to take my hand when I steered around a corner. One time, I turned into a neighbor's driveway for a joke. I can't laugh like that now."

"It's only been three weeks."

Casey got a blank look on his face, and he looked out the door, onto Bingo's main street. A UPS truck went by. He drank his tea. "I hate that color of brown. The phone rings. A sound in a vast cave. I can't think of anyone I want to talk to. My sons are too busy to call, of course."

Lou sipped his coffee and looked at his friend, wrinkled clothes, bags under his eyes.

"People drop off food, but I can't eat. I can't sleep. Then, in my dreams still, huge women chase me, tearing my clothes off. I'm crying, 'Lily, Lily' at the top of my lungs." Casey sipped his tea. "This may be an overshare."

"I'm good, so far."

"I'm not mad at you. Maybe at god or that vicious bacteria. Maybe Lily, for falling and then dying. With the sleeplessness, sometimes Lily seems so close. I can feel her and talk to her."

"Maybe she has more free time now." Lou chewed his blueberry muffin.

Casey laughed, a little longer than was necessary. "I like that. What could she be busy with? Where the hell is she?"

A young couple at a nearby table turned towards Casey's outburst.

"Okay." He quieted down. "Are you ready for weird? I told you about Angela. Of course I did... you know."

"Yeah. Hard to forget."

"You do listen sometimes. Last night I finally listened to my messages. The director of the service had called me the day before Lily's death to say that he didn't have any coverage for me for a few days. He called me the day Lily died, to apologize that he was looking but no helpers for that day, either."

"There's different Hospices, right?"

"No. Listen to me. Where did Angela come from?"

"Half the women in Mexico are named Angela."

"I'm just saying, who was at my house? I called the director this morning. I'd like to find her."

"Hey, Casey, good to see you. Long time." Lou's friend Patricia balanced a coffee cup, a bagel and a newspaper in one hand, while she dragged a chair up to the table. "I'm so sorry about Lily. She passed on at a perfect time. I did her chart. Pluto opened the door for her. He's right behind the New moon. Birth, death."

"What are you talking about?" Casey asked.

"Isn't Pluto the loneliest planet?" Lou asked. "Farthest from the sun."

"No need to grieve. Lily is always with you. I talk to a lot of dead people. Some I'm still doing their charts. I thought maybe I could join you, help you. I always say 'transformed into light' when I'm talking about the dead. Dying is so physical." She reached out and took Casey's hand.

"So real," Lou said. Patricia's effort at support, within her framework of eccentric spiritual beliefs, bothered Lou. He decided Casey could take care of himself.

"And with the great sun of transformation blazing in a new sky, the laws of nature are temporarily revoked," she said.

"Really," Casey responded. After a pause, he continued. "Listening to you, Patricia, I just get angrier and angrier."

"Okay," Patricia said.

"Okay," Casey said. "Okay. You're right. I'm taking a deep breath."

"That's good," Patricia replied.

"Yes, a strange thing happened with Hospice..."

"Angela?"

"How did you…"

"That's why I sat down with you. I was helping my neighbor go into the light. She had all these people, services, nurses coming and going. And then this Central American woman from Hospice came in for the last days. I called the company to thank them. They had never heard of her. She was a saint in a weird native hat, all feathers and rags. She was so kind, and I felt that she had suffered a lot."

"That's right. The hat. Lou thinks I am crazy. But you saw her."

"Yes, I met her. A short, thin woman, spoke almost no English."

Chapter 19

How Lou's Gay Neighbors Met

"No, I want to go. Mrs. Dal said that if we cultivate diverse types of people, we mythologize our own existence."

"What does that mean?" Jennie had been resistant to the last lunch plan with Freddie and Tommie.

"We can live our lives like they were myths."

"Okay." Lou appreciated Jennie's enthusiasm, but had no idea what she was talking about.

"Like Prometheus, the quest for fire. Fire is like transformation, intelligence."

"Okay."

"So, Freddie and Tommie are transforming culture, just by living together, their own myth, creating a diverse future for all of us."

"Okay."

"Cool. Dad, you can be so dense, but I think there's hope for you." Jennie came over to the counter where Lou was washing dishes and gave him a big hug.

"I like that," Lou said.

"So, lunch is research," she continued. "Into what Tommie and Freddie lived through. People died for their right to have sex. Stonestown..."

"That's the Mall in San Francisco, sweetie."

"Stonewall? See, I have to ask them about it."

"Well, I went to a gay bar once by accident. I wanted to watch a ball game. Aren't there gay kids at your school?"

"Of course. But Freddie and Tommie are old, like you. Plus, every once in a while, I want to do something to make you happy." Lou's heart expanded until it almost burst.

Half an hour later, they were eating lunch. Frederick the Great ran around the table, barking happily and continuously. Lou looked at the dog, then at Tommie, but the barking continued.

"Have you seen that hunky-looking young man on the property?" Tommie asked.

"He creeps me out," Jennie said, after she swallowed a spoonful of soup.

"Uh oh," Freddie asked. "He's so thrilling, with the angry look and the leather jacket. The young Marlon Brando."

"He's too thin," Tommie said.

"Who?" Lou asked.

"A young man who apparently lives in the Orchard now," Freddie said.

"I'm with Jennie," Tommie said. "He's a lit stick of dynamite. I don't want to be there when..."

"Let's talk about Fido," Jennie interrupted. Lou was surprised by her interjection.

"Beautiful segue, my dear. Our favorite topic," Freddie said. He sipped his tea. "We were both at the San Rafael pound on the same day. It was fate. Dog pound. Sounds violent, don't you think?"

"I was looking for love," Tommie said. "You were looking for a dog."

"How dare you?" Freddie rejoined. "I had just gotten over losing my Jackie. What a hunk he was."

"Sometimes I want a dog," Jennie said. *Really,* Lou thought. *The things that come out of her mouth.*

"I'll tell it now, love," Tommie said. "I had taken care of Richard for two years, day and night. All the people bringing food, they could get on with their lives. And they did. But I couldn't. Richard's sister suggested that I go to this dog shelter. Now, I had my eye on Frederick the Great, the sweetest little dog. The loneliness was unendurable."

Jennie's shirt was covered with blueberry pie stains. Lou loved her enthusiastic eating until he did her laundry. At that moment, Frederick barked again happily from his elaborate doggie bed under the dining room table. And barked. Tommie took a deep breath.

"Gosh, so much death. I'm so sorry," Jennie said. "So sorry."

"Truly," Freddie said. "A lot of us thought we would never survive. The Castro was like a war zone, funerals every week. I lost Jackie just when we thought we were safe. So catastrophic.

So sudden."

He paused for a moment and wiped his eyes. "Oh, Jackie. Tommie..."

"Of course." Tommie picked up the story. "This must be eight years ago..."

Freddie wiped his eyes and interrupted. "Eight and a half, dear."

Tommie took a deep breath. "I saw a little dog with all the life force in the world. I needed someone to fill the empty place in my heart. I told the staff to hold Frederick for me. I needed to go to the store for a doggie bed, food, etc. But when I arrived back at the shelter, oh my god, he was gone. I ran out into the parking lot, yelling and screaming."

"And that's how we met," Freddie said. He patted Tommie on the hand. "I had Frederick the Great in my car, snuggled into his new doggie bed."

"The bed I bought was much better and showed that I wanted him more. Oh, you should have seen the fur fly, and the yelling."

"Well, of course, it was all Tommie's fault. If he had..."

"It was your fault, sir. And I beg you to understand. I cannot be corrected like this in front of my friends."

"Our friends. There you go. Do you know how stupid you appear in public? How stupid that makes me feel?"

Both men were standing beside the table loaded with pie plates and teacups, yelling at each other. "My dog, my dog."

Frederick the Great jumped up on the table and knocked over a teacup. Tommie grabbed him and held him close.

"I think we should go now," Lou said.

"I almost finished my pie," Jennie said.

All of a sudden, the two men calmed down. Freddie grabbed Tommie in a big hug.

"Oh you big, angry hunk. I just love your joie de vivre, your authenticity. Yes, come here and give me a kiss."

Tommie and Freddie embraced. Frederick the Great circled them, still yapping.

Freddie turned towards Lou and Jennie, and said, "No, stay. We are fine. Tommie gets like this."

"Freddie," Tommie warned.

"Tommie," Freddie said. "Hey, I want them to see your coat."

"The coat. Okay, dear." Tommie relaxed. He came back in a few minutes wearing a shiny, full-length leather overcoat.

"Isn't he beautiful?" Freddie said. "I bought that for him after you told the story, Jennie. He's my hero."

"Look. It's emblazoned with my name in black leather thread over this pocket," Tommie said. "You have to look closely."

Jennie said, "I love your coat." She looked at Lou.

"I bought this to go with it," Tommie said. He went over to the coat rack behind the front door and put on a leather hat with a brim.

"Isn't he gorgeous?" Freddie asked. "Now you can go, if you must. Such a pleasure." Frederick the Great started barking again, sharp and insistent, leaping at Lou's feet.

"They seem to really care about each other," Jennie said as she and Lou walked back to their cabin. "After all that loss."

They walked through the battered cabins at the Orchard, and Lou could hear the creek in the distance. He loved his daughter's openness about their friends' relationship.

"Sieg heil," she said.

"What?" Lou said.

"It's so weird to see gay people in Nazi-style regalia. Plus, I hate dogs like that," Jennie said.

"Me too."

Chapter 20

Lou and Yarrow Go for a Ride

Lou drove slowly along the winding road. Though the weather was cold, he had rolled down the window. Redwood needles covered the cracked asphalt, and the creek roared down in the narrow canyon.

"Mom put you up to this," Yarrow said.

Lou tightened up a little. How did kids figure out so much?

The first thirty minutes of their drive to Pt. Reyes had passed in complete silence. Lou drank from his water bottle.

"Yes, she did. I had the same idea."

"Maybe I believe you. But it's okay. I wanted to talk to you."

There was something breathless and rough about the way Yarrow spoke. Maybe his voice was changing.

"April said something about your grades. And your father."

"He wouldn't notice me if I set myself on fire."

Lou swore. "Goddamn these bikers. I'm in a truck, by the way," He slowed down, waiting to pass in a narrow part of the road through the redwoods.

"Yeah, they should have made the road straight."

Lou laughed.

"Mom sure knows how to pick partners."

"What's that supposed to mean?"

"You're all so sensitive and talk about spending quality time with me." Yarrow made air quotes around 'quality time.' "You're not staying, so what difference does it make?"

"How come everyone but me knows whether I'm staying or going?"

"She runs everyone off," Yarrow said. "I could care less, FYI."

Silence returned to the truck. The light slanting through the redwoods seemed full of magic to Lou. It comforted him.

"What do you mean, 'she runs everyone off'?" Lou said after a few minutes.

"You don't know yet?" Yarrow looked out the window. "She chases people till they run off."

"People?"

"Like you," Yarrow said. Silence settled in the truck. Lou listened to the creek while he drove.

"Tell me," Yarrow finally said. "Why should I care about math and history? What a waste. You didn't finish college, right?"

"No."

"See."

"See what? I'm a handyman, Yarrow."

"No. You're an artist. That's what I think. I want my own destiny, not be a cubicle man like my father. He's happy when he gets a bigger office. I want to right wrongs and save fair damsels. My form of art."

"You must be in that class with Jennie."

"Yes, Mrs. Dal makes us believe that we're all bigger than our family history and our DNA."

"Jennie says that. I need a translation." *Finally, they had something to talk about*, Lou thought.

"It's hard to explain. You're maybe like a wandering hero, one foot at the bus stop and the other on a banana peel."

Lou laughed. "I don't need a bus when my truck is running."

"Seriously, dude, why would anyone get tied down to Bingo, a partner, a mortgage? I can't drive yet."

"You're what, fourteen now, son?"

"You don't get to call me that."

"I meant it in a mythic way."

"I know when I'm being patronized." Yarrow banged his hand down on the dashboard. "Pull over and let me out."

The narrow road had opened up into rolling hills, and Lou found a place to park.

Yarrow reached for the door handle. Lou turned off his engine and said, "Stay here. Give me five minutes."

In the background, the creek rustled over large and small stones. Lou liked Yarrow. He couldn't remember his father taking him for a ride, just to talk.

Yarrow settled back in his seat.

"No one wants to go off on their own."

"Odysseus pretends he's crazy, but he finally goes to Troy to war."

"Right. I left my hometown because I had to."

"See, that's your myth…"

"Okay. Some part of me was going to die if I stayed. But leaving is just as hard, going to places with no friends, no history."

"Soul death if you stay where you were born. Isn't that what your story is telling me?"

Lou rubbed his face. April wasn't going to like his talk with Yarrow, if he stopped here.

"Yarrow, you have things here I never had. Friends, a mother who cares about you, a good school."

Yarrow's voice became more insistent. "You don't get it. American white bread middle class. I want more. I don't know what it is. But who am I here? A fourteen-year-old with everything and nothing at the same time. The definition of hell."

"Like I said…"

"Five minutes is up." Yarrow got out of the truck and slammed the door. "You're no Odysseus."

Lou rolled down the window and said, "Dinner's at six."

The sound of the creek always soothed him. It flowed down to the bay, through the oaks and redwoods, following its natural course. *Yarrow's a good kid,* he thought.

He drove and felt the old road bounding under his wheels. He imagined it connecting with all the highways in the country.

Chapter 21

A Grain of Rice

"The group leader. Comes on so touchy-feely. But he's recruiting me. He needs more mentors for the Hospice program."

"Who would want to recruit you?" Lou asked. Casey shot a look at him. "Just kidding."

"You think I'm angry? I am. What am I supposed to do?"

"Live?"

"Shut up and let me finish my taco. You need the Hospice training, son."

"Not likely."

"You think you're not going to die?"

Lou and Casey sat on Casey's porch, on a warm, humid winter evening. Jennie and some friends were jumping their skateboards off a homemade ramp in the street.

"I hate that clash," Casey said.

"It's Jennie and her friends."

"I know. I know. Feels like a big storm coming."

"I love the sound of the creek."

"Wait till it's in your living room."

"Floods, noisy kids. You're a cheery one."

Casey brought out a couple of beers and set them on a wicker table next to a bowl of chips.

"At the group, people say anger is part of grieving. They are right. I keep getting angrier and angrier."

"Okay."

"Fourteen women and two men. Bunch of morons. I wished more of the women had died and their partners were there."

"Nice," Lou said, sipping his beer.

"All that Kleenex. These women are like vultures circling their prey. At the break, three of them wanted to go out for coffee with me."

"You told me no one would want to go out with you."

"You don't need to remind me."

Out on the street, brakes screeched and a man yelled. Lou sat up, then relaxed. He thought, I don't have to do anything till there's blood on the concrete.

"After break, the director tells this story. A woman comes to the Buddha and says, 'My son died. How could this have happened? Please help me.'" Casey paused and ate a couple of chips. "The Buddha says, 'I can help you. First, go into your village and get a grain of rice from each family that has never experienced the kind of grief you feel. Bring me a bowl of such rice and then we can talk.' The lady came back the next week and said, 'I couldn't find any of that rice. Thank you.' And she went away."

Lou chewed his chips and noticed how the street noise had quieted. He felt Casey's anguish, his anger. Lou was happy to sit with him, as the night settled in, with the creek rushing by the cabin.

"The woman going to all the houses. Wasn't she angry? Then I looked at the people in the group. Their loss was as terrible as mine. Their son. Their husband. For a moment, I became the woman hearing all the stories of loss. I still felt like crap, but something welled up in my chest like a hot wave. The love I used to feel coming at me from Lily was gone forever. I felt desolate. Like no one would ever love me like that, and I was lost and then the wave broke on my face and I cried and cried. I put my face in my hands and cried.

"The director came across the circle and tried to hug me. I totally lost it. I yelled, 'She's not coming back. Never, never, never. I don't want a grain of rice. I want Lily.' I jumped up and kicked over a chair as I walked out. I sat in my car. I was so mad, I was shaking. But then it was like the storm had passed. The grief had left and there was a kind of peace."

"Poetic," Lou said. He sipped his beer and listened to the creek in the background.

"I'm trying here. This weird peace filled the car. I wasn't angry anymore. It was like Lily was there with me, and she was saying, 'It's going to be all right.' If any of those morons at the Hospice meeting had said that, I would have blown a fuse. But I looked up at the mountain and I thought, Well, okay. Maybe so."

Casey sipped his beer and glanced out into the street. One of the neighbors drove by in his Subaru Outback and waved. Casey raised his bottle in salute. "His life goes on. Mine too."

Lou said, "I've been thinking about Julie lately. When she died, where did she go? Why did she leave me with Jennie? It's weird to live in this world and know she's gone. I can remember, like an old song on the radio, the way I used to care for her. Maybe that's grief, I don't know. I'm glad Jennie's here, now. Getting more rooted in Bingo."

"That makes it harder for you to go, yeah? Do you want more chips or beer?"

"Just chips."

Casey returned from the kitchen and Lou clinked bottles with him.

Casey was quiet a moment. "Thanks for coming over, Lou. You know what?"

"What?"

"It's going to be all right."

Lou looked out into the roaring creek. Then he looked at his friend and said, "Maybe so." He thought about the big storm coming.

Chapter 22

The Flood

"Dad, wake up, wake up. I'm cold."

Lou was deep in the dream again. His father yelled at him. He couldn't find the keys to his truck, and then his father set it on fire. He woke up, rattled.

"What?" he yelled again. "What?"

The rain roared on the shake roof.

Lou had fallen asleep in front of the computer, tracking the upstream flows in the creek. The rain had been pounding continually for five days. The weather service had predicted the water would go over the banks. But when? His neck hurt.

"I'll make a fire."

"No service," Jennie said, shaking her phone. "Nothing around here works."

"It's the country, sweetheart."

"I wanted to leave that shit behind." She stood by the wood stove, rubbing her hands together. "That's better."

The storm had knocked out the electricity three days earlier. The creek, close behind the cabins, was filling ominously. Old-timers in the neighborhood remembered water coming through the property, muddy and tree-filled.

Lou warmed himself at the fire and thought of his days in Humboldt, when the winter rain had come like a fierce animal. Its brutal force had sent redwoods crashing down on the narrow roads. One time, he drove down US 101, through pieces of shattered redwood as large as his truck.

"The water is coming over the banks," she said. "I'm scared."

"I'm glad April went home."

"I wish we had gone with her," Jennie said. "What do we do?"

"We talked about this last night."

"Now it's for real."

"Maybe."

The rain banged on the roof. Nature could be so furious. Lou felt very small, helpless in its grip. Where could he go to be safe, where could he take his daughter? Some atavistic fear gripped his stomach.

"We're fine, Jennie. We're fine. Look, the house is three feet higher than the parking lot."

"I want to get out of here. Look out the window."

A wide, muddy stream flowed across the parking lot. Lou's piles of recycled redwood boards were covered with a foot of water, and they started to shift. Sticks and branches moved through the water.

"Let's listen to the little blue radio," he said. "If it says we evacuate, we evacuate."

The constant thud of rain almost drowned out the voice on the solar-powered radio. Then they heard a voice on a loudspeaker, coming from outside the cabin.

"What the fuck?" Lou asked.

"He's up on the road," Jennie said. "But I can't hear him. It looks like a sheriff's car."

They finally heard the man. "Folks in the Orchard, it's time to go. Get out, now."

"Shit, okay," Lou said. "Get your bag." He looked around the cabin. Everything seemed so fragile, impermanent.

"I feel so cold, like the rain put out my internal heat."

"That's fear. Just do the next thing. Get your bag." Lou put a hand on Jennie's shoulder. "You're trembling."

"Uh, yeah."

Casey came up on the porch, covered in rain gear from head to toe. He carried a wet backpack and a walking stick.

"Did you hear the sheriff?" Lou asked. "Do you need any help?"

"No. My car is up on the road, like your truck. Getting to it will be fun."

"Anyone else in the Orchard?"

"Everyone's gone but Luke. Well, his truck is in the parking lot, up to the hubcaps in water. I gotta go. We all gotta go."

Casey turned to leave and Lou said, "We'll meet you at the cars. Be careful."

"Dad."

"Okay, get your pack."

Jennie stuffed her phone into her backpack and zipped it up.

"Come on, honey."

Lou and Jennie walked carefully down a rain-slick hill and into the parking area. Water had surged up to the door of Luke's battered Ford truck. Casey waved from above, by the road.

"Hold my hand," Lou said, repositioning his pack on his back. As they stepped into the fast-moving creek, the water rose six inches. Lou felt an insistent pressure on his side, pushing him downstream. The water rose over his waist.

Jennie yelled, "Dad!"

Lou pulled her close to him, but a small, uprooted apple tree limb hit him in the back. He lurched and lost his footing.

"Jennie!" Lou shouted. He felt the current pull her hand out of his. "Jennie!" Tangled in tree limbs, he watched as she slipped and went underwater. Her head came out of the water and she screamed.

"Dad!" He could hardly hear her over the tumultuous thunder of the water. She was so close, but a wall of water surged at him.

Where was she? Lou threw down his pack and stepped over and under thick tree limbs. He looked frantically left and right.

No Jennie. He saw her pack floating off downstream and started stumbling towards it. More trees came down in the flooding creek. One crashed into the truck, and Lou heard Jennie scream. She was clinging to an outside mirror. Four feet of water pushed her under the truck.

"Dad!"

"Hold on."

Lou fought his way free of the branches, then ducked as another tree limb went over his head. He could hardly move upstream towards Jennie. He moved step by step. He stumbled on a loose rock and almost fell.

"Dad, Dad."

Lou grabbed a long stick that was floating by and supported himself with it. Testing each step, he moved slowly towards her.

"Hold on." He lost his balance and fell back a few steps.

Jennie yelled, "Dad!" He finally reached her and took her arm.

In his truck, up on the bank finally, Lou turned on the heater.

"That was scary."

"True that."

"You're strong, Jennie. I love you. You need dry clothes."

Jennie shivered. Her long hair hung down across her wet tee shirt. "Yeah, can you go back and get me some?"

They both laughed. The creek roared by below them.

Casey tapped on Lou's window. "You made it."

"Yeah."

"Good for you. I'm going to go get warm somewhere."

"Okay."

Through the crashing rain, Lou and Jennie could just barely make out their cabin. Luke's truck was starting to rock slightly in the current.

"Johnie said the cabins are relatively flood-proof, that they had been there a long time," Lou said. The car heater was doing its job.

"If the rain ever stops," Jennie said. "That was great."

"What?"

"Like Mrs. Dal said, 'Life is epic.'"

"This is our little ark, then," Lou said, waving at the inside of his truck.

"Well, you know why Noah collected the animals two by two?" Jennie asked.

Lou looked over at her.

"That's seriously gross," he said.

"Sorry. I didn't mean ... Can we go now?"

"Did you bring your homework?"

Chapter 23

Jennie's Fall

"**A**re you vegetarian today?" Lou asked. Tired after a long day changing pipes under a house, he was throwing together a quick taco dinner for Jennie and himself.

"Totally vegan. But you could put in a little of that chicken, Dad," Jennie said.

'Dad.' After several months, Lou was still getting used to that word.

Jennie got her backpack tangled in her red and purple hair when she took it off. "Shit, this thing is so heavy."

"Language," he said, hopelessly, as he set two plates on the kitchen table.

"I'm so glad it stopped raining," Jennie said. "How long are you going to sleep on the couch, anyway? I feel weird in your room, stumbling over your funky tools and shit. Ah, sorry."

"What's that bruise on your arm?"

"You don't know if we're going to stay, so why get a bigger house? Is that what you're thinking? Pull me out of high school. Hit the road like Jack fucking Kerouac."

"Ah, language, please. BTW, I'm okay on the couch."

"For now. Is April? I know when you borrow 'my' room." Jennie made air quotes.

"Your arm?"

Jennie turned away from him. "Ah, I fell."

"Is someone bullying you?"

"Hell, no. I collided with a kid."

Jennie speed-chewed her taco and wiped some salsa off her lower lip. She rubbed her shin at the same time. Lou saw a wide white bandage through a hole in her jeans.

"Let me see that."

"It's fine."

"Let me see."

"No. It's fine."

After dinner, Lou got his first aid box out of the truck.

Jennie sat on the toilet and rolled up her pants leg. Lou sat on the tub next to her. "You could perform surgery with that gear," she said.

"I have. One time, a guy nail-gunned his foot to the floor. I never drank beer at lunch again."

"Good call, Dad. I think I hit my head a little."

"Oh shit."

"Language, Dad. It's fine. No headaches. No twitches."

"Hold tight," he said as he yanked the bandage off her leg. Jennie screamed. "Ow, ow."

"Had to be done, sorry." Lou unscrewed a bottle of hydrogen peroxide.

"No."

"Yes. Who cleaned it?"

"After the crash, all the kids were laughing, taking pictures of me sitting on the curb, and posting my fall on Instagram. Bunch of dicks. Ouch. Then this Hispanic woman comes up, wearing a weird hat with carpet hanging off it. She takes a couple of handy wipes out of a huge bag that looked like a sewn-up rug. Ouch. Dad."

"Sorry. I have to get out a little piece of gravel."

"It feels like you hit the bone."

"I'm glad she was there." Lou dropped a cotton swab into the wastebasket.

"She puts her arms around me and asks me where my mother is. Then I really dropped a puddle on her. I hadn't cried that hard since the funeral. Wah-wah-wah. I untangled myself after a while. I felt happy. I mean, my leg hurt but I felt peaceful. I reached for my skateboard and then she was gone. Like she got beamed up or something."

"Ouch again. You're used to cleaning up guys."

Lou laughed. "They don't flinch." He turned to the sink to wash his hands.

"Thanks, Dad. You're the best."

She gave him a quick kiss that rocked his heart. Where did these intense feelings of love and fear come from? With a sense of awe, he watched her walk out of the bathroom. She had come from him?

He asked, "Do vegetarians eat ice cream?" He waved a container he had taken out of the freezer.

"Vegan, Dad. There's a big difference. And yes. Dairy-free ice cream."

"No such thing as dairy-free ice cream."

"Okay." Jennie read the label. "This looks good. You actually shop for me. That's so awesome."

"It's my job. Supply a massive amount of food…"

"You're great at it, Dad." Jennie continued her story, as she licked her spoon. "At first, when this woman helped me, I felt, like, so warm. Nice touch with the handy wipes. When I was sitting next to her on the curb, like, a part of me could just lean into her, let down. Go soft. Right?"

"Sure."

"But then she disappeared so suddenly. I felt angry and I slammed my skateboard down on the ground. Yarrow came over to help me, and I said, 'Where did the lady go?' He said, 'What lady?' 'The lady who put the bandage on, nut ball,' I said. Is that weird or what? Yarrow never saw her."

"He was looking at his phone?"

"I felt angry till I got home and saw you heating up my tacos."

Chapter 24

Lou Finally Meets His New Neighbor

After pricing out a job, Lou came home early to grab a bite to eat. He smelled cigarette smoke as he entered his cabin. Then he heard someone in the back yard.

"Hey," he yelled.

A thin man in a red flannel shirt ran down the narrow foot path that led deeper into the Orchard community.

Lou followed and yelled, "Hey. Hey."

He followed the man through the trees, along a mostly unused path to a battered cabin set back in the forest.

Lou knocked on the front door. No one answered.

"Open the fucking door."

Finally, the man in the red flannel shirt came to the screen door, rubbing his eyes and yawning. A horned animal was tattooed on the back of his right hand.

"You were in my house."

"Who the fuck are you?"

"The guy who's telling you to keep out of my house. Now get the fuck out of the way. I'm going to see if you stole anything."

The man grabbed the inside handle of the screen door. With his other hand he pulled a long knife out of a scabbard on his belt.

"Fuck you. I've been sleeping."

"Why are you breathing hard?"

"I was jacking off, asshole. Get off my porch."

Both men let go of the screen door. Lou took a deep breath. He wasn't twenty anymore.

"Someone who looked exactly like you just jumped off my porch and ran in here."

"My evil twin," the man said and laughed. "Yeah, my evil twin. My Uncle Johnie asked me to help him out. The guy he hired is a big fuck-up. I'm thinking that's you. I'll be in your house and in your face. I'm taking over."

"If anything is missing, I'll be back here."

"Fuck you. You can settle it like a man, right now. Or be a pussy."

"Aren't you the pussy who ran away when I came home?" Lou watched himself getting riled up. He felt younger and quite stupid. Who was this punk? Lou took a deep breath and turned to go.

"Jennie lives there, right? You think you can protect her, don't you? Good luck with that, pussy man. Pussy daddy. After I get things settled here, she's going to Oregon with me. She told me. She's tired of you."

"We'll see," Lou said as he walked off the porch. He was shaking with rage, and went directly to Johnie's rambling farmhouse.

Johnie came to the door. "What are you so angry about?" He held a beer can, and in the background, Lou heard the sounds of a football game.

"That little prick in the forest."

"Shit, what did he do?"

"He was in my house."

"Shit. My cousin asked me to put him up for a while. Give him some work."

"My job?"

"No, no. I need you, Lou."

"He was in my house."

"I'll talk to him."

"I just tried that."

"He's a little headstrong. But he's family. Give him a chance."

"I already did. I have a daughter, Johnie. I don't want him in my house, and he's not working with me."

"He just has to stay out of trouble for a few more months."

"He's on probation, right? Fuck you, Johnie."

"Fuck you right back. I'm doing my cousin a favor. I'm going back to the game." Johnie went into the house towards the sound of the television.

Chapter 25

Casey Volunteers for Hospice

"Are you sure you want to do this?" Lou was driving Casey to his first volunteer assignment – an elderly man who had lost his son and his wife.

Casey replied, "I could stay home and watch the paint dry."

"I meant have me come along."

"Just keep your mouth shut at the appointment. I need a driver."

"Did you have to make the appointment at night?" Lou asked. "In the day, you could drive yourself."

"Maybe I didn't want to go alone. The trainer said I was ready, that I connect with the grieving people. Okay, I can give it a try."

"But?"

"Maybe it's early for me to get an assignment, you know?"

"Okay."

"After twilight, sitting alone is hell. I think of things I said to her. Why wasn't I kinder?"

Good question, Lou thought. He slowed down to look at a street sign in the dark. "Is this Laurel?"

"How should I know? This poor bastard lost a son and a wife."

Lou found a little house whose porch light was out and he parked. They knocked, then heard a loud TV go off. A tall, thin man in a dirty blue sweater opened the door.

"You're Erik?" Casey asked.

"Yeah." Erik shuffled a little as he ushered them into a living room that smelled of stale air and burnt coffee.

"Something to drink?" Erik asked.

"Water is fine," Lou said. Casey nodded. He took out some papers and handouts as Erik returned with three glasses of water on a tray.

"I looked at that already," Erik said. "Tell me where to sign, and then go."

"There's a little protocol we follow," Casey said. He leaned towards Erik and held out a clipboard with some documents on it. Erik sat motionless in his worn leather chair.

"I didn't know you were bringing someone."

Casey sat back in his lumpy chair. "Sorry. I left you a voice mail and email."

"What's the fucking point of checking the phone machine?"

"I know what that's like," Casey said.

"Do you? Do you?" Erik sounded shrill, angry. Casey took a deep breath.

"Your application says that you want an occasional visitor, maybe some help with housework and shopping. Anything else?"

"You have to have a reason to go on, right?"

"That's up to you," Casey said. "I'm on the Bereavement team."

"Bereavement." Erik snorted. "Great. Do you two get matching uniforms when you finish your training?"

"It's part of grieving, sorrow and anger all mixed..."

"Some asshole t-bones my wife and son. I'm so fucking weak and old that I need a ride down the hill. I want to kill him and can't. Is that anger or sorrow?"

Lou looked around the house again. Pictures of Erik with an older woman; pictures of a young Erik, with a full head of dark brown hair, throwing a ball to a young boy in a baseball uniform, swinging a bat.

"Are you having thoughts of harming yourself?" Casey asked in a soft voice.

"Are you listening? I said 'Kill him,' not me." Erik pushed the papers around on his little table and shrugged.

Lou felt the night, strong and dark, pressing down on the little house in the hills. The forest brooded at the end of the road. Up in the hills, deer lay in thick manzanita brush for a few moments of safety and rest with their fawns.

For Erik, he thought, there would be no rest from the relentless fact: his family was gone.

For a moment, Lou felt his heart open, to all the people like Erik, sorrowing this night, in towns and cities across America, parents mourning children, children mourning parents.

So many tears, so many angry, heart-broken people. All for love, all for love.

Casey put down his papers and looked out the window.

"I get more conversation watching the grass grow, than with you two," Erik said. "I'm too weak to cut the goddamned grass and I'll be damned if I'll pay someone to take care of it. It's not my house anymore if I can't fix it up."

"What?" Casey said.

Erik stared at him while Casey pulled together a stack of papers.

Now Erik looked out into the darkness. "Some part of my brain is missing. I don't want any of this shit now. Can you leave?"

Casey continued. "Maybe you're ashamed of being an asshole to your wife. I know what that's like. Maybe that's why you're so angry."

"Shut the hell up. What do you know?"

"I know how to be an asshole, but you could give lessons. Lily, that's my wife, or she was. She was no angel. I mean, I loved her but I could get off the rails with her. You know, yell, swear."

"Mister, that's the one true thing either of you said in here. The rest is just a shitstorm of fake consolation. I said it's time for you to leave. My home is my prison. Solitary confinement. Who am I? No parent. No husband."

"You're a morose old fucker, aren't you? If you ever thought of something outside of your little tragedy, you might feel better."

Lou pulled Casey out the door.

As they walked down the broken sidewalk towards his truck, Lou said, "You know it's only been ten days for him."

"Still."

"Still nothing. Listen to yourself."

They got into Lou's truck, and he wove silently down the darkened streets.

"I know Erik so well. But I can't help him. My home no longer feels like my home either. Maybe I'm the angry fucker."

"Maybe," Lou said. He drove down the hill.

Chapter 26

Jennie Finds Her Voice

"You look wrecked," April said.

"I had the dream," Lou responded. "I've got to go somewhere. My truck is full of carvings of animals. My father sets it on fire. He shakes the keys at me but won't give them to me. Plus, getting up early so Jennie is comfortable."

"I heard you pacing out here."

April drank her coffee. "That dream won't leave you alone."

"Like it's my friend but it won't let me sleep."

"It's getting to be our friend. You said you had it as a child. "

"A hundred times. More."

"It's trying to tell you something."

"Okay. What?"

"I don't know."

She and Lou were eating breakfast on a warm spring morning, out on his deck. Bulb shoots were breaking through the packed mud left over from the flood. A lone, long-winged egret flew up the creek, still running with a trickle of water.

"He's a long way from home," Lou said.

April arched an eyebrow and Lou laughed.

"I didn't say a word."

"I feel like shit. Just one good night's sleep."

"You were telling me about some Guatemalan lady who helped Jennie?" April asked.

"Yeah, she bandaged Jennie's knee after a fall." Lou looked out at the rippling water in the creek.

"Something else?" April sipped her tea and waited.

"Jennie cried when she told me. Got me thinking about Jennie and her mother. I'm no mother."

"True that."

"Barely a father."

"You keep her fed and in school. Don't underestimate…"

"Okay."

"The woman sounds like Angela. She's been volunteering on the school lunch grounds the last few days. Kids sit around eating pizza and listening to her."

"How do you know it's her?"

Lou wasn't looking forward to a hard day under a house, taking iron drainpipes apart, so a few extra minutes in the fresh air felt good. He liked talking with April.

"That hat you described, feathers, fabric, on a fat Guatemalan. Sorry, large. It's hard to be P.C. all the time."

"No shit."

"It's weird to watch the kids with her. No phones, no texting."

"I wish I could keep Jennie's attention."

"You do okay. So, Angela talks about Jesus and the Dalai Lama as if they had coffee with her. Teachers gather in little clumps with their arms crossed. She is upsetting the administration. In afternoon classes, the kids won't settle down. Suddenly, they want meaning, to talk about what they believe in."

"That's all her fault, I guess. No wonder the teachers are worried," Lou added. "Except you, of course. You're all about meaning."

"I think that's a compliment."

Lou kissed April goodbye and started loading his tools into his truck. What did he believe in? Was there a story of Jesus, or Buddha, or Stalin or Martin Luther King that moved him? That would make the dream go away? He was so tired.

His love for Jennie astonished him, moved him, mostly to anxiety. Who was she going to become? How could he prevent himself from totally fucking her up? Every week she stayed, it was harder to leave Bingo. School activities, friends, acting class. Plus April.

"All the cool kids were wandering through the halls, saying it was time for a protest, free speech and all that," Jennie said when she got home late from school, excited and sweaty. "We had just studied the Boston Tea Party."

Lou put two plates of fish tacos on the little wooden table in the kitchen while Jennie put away her backpack and washed up. He said, "Time to what?"

"Are you listening, Dad? To walk out. Here's this perfectly nice person, talking to us. The administration called the police. But Dad, the students surrounded the two cops who came. Angela kept saying, 'I can go; puedo ir. Something like that. No problemo.' We started throwing food at the police."

"We?"

"Ah, I followed her but didn't throw food."

Lou didn't believe her. "Did you walk out during classes?" He enjoyed both his taco and the enthusiastic look he saw on his daughter's face.

"Well, duh. It wouldn't be a walk-out after classes end, would it? It was like the first time I made a stand for something. Angela should be able to talk without the police state descending on her."

"We're a long way from a police state, honey."

"Whatever." Jennie chewed her taco. "This is good, by the way. Mom couldn't heat water."

"Thanks. So you had your own revolution."

"Don't be sarcastic. The police evicted her from campus. That's bullshit. A big crowd of students followed her down the middle of the street. It wasn't our fault that the traffic got stopped up and the police had to come back."

"Okay."

"Honest, Dad, you should go and see her talk. I think you'd get something out of it. Angela believes in things, invisible things, miracles, and ethics…"

"And I don't."

"You never say you do. Is this all there is?" Jennie motioned around the little cabin. "Books, dirty clothes, homework. I want more. I want to believe in more."

Lou remembered such passions. They were why he'd gone back to the land with Julie, why they'd had a daughter.

"We sat in the park for a few hours. There was something different about Angela. I think having all these people follow her … I don't know. She talked for a long time and no one moved. We were sitting by this huge tulip tree that was in full bloom, like all the kids were blooming too, becoming something different. Then Angela stood up and kind of disappeared. She didn't walk away, she was just gone, again. I don't know how she does it."

"Jennie, I got tear-gassed a couple of times, when I was

standing up for something. It's not fun."

"You never told me that. But I bet you felt like I did, alive. Like I learned more about myself this afternoon than in the last year.'

"Which was…"

Lou was washing dishes. He wished he had time to do his invoices. No billing, no money. He thought, Yeah, what happened to my dream? I'm a handyman for people whose houses are falling down.

Jennie was quiet as she pulled books and folders out of her backpack. "You're not listening, Dad. You had to be there. Something happened today."

Chapter 27

Casey Turns Towards Healing

"Yo, Casey."

His friend turned slowly from his seat at the Coffee Heaven. "You're too old for 'yo,' Lou."

"Jennie lets me practice with her."

Spring light slanted through the tall windows of the coffee shop with a reddish, early-morning gleam. His ceramic coffee cup glinted. Nothing else sat on his little round table, no paper, no magazine. After he welcomed Lou with a half-hearted smile, Casey returned to an inert state.

"Can I sit down?"

"I'm about as good a companion as a tombstone."

"What's new about that?" Lou asked.

"I could sit here all day. No one would give a shit."

"Until closing. Let's take a walk."

"Yeah, yeah, yeah."

The morning air felt fresh, as the two friends walked. Narcissus bulbs pushed their way up towards the sun in a grassy strip by the town ballpark.

"I had a dream about Lily. She was standing in this big river. She was gesturing to me, 'Come on, come on.' Light was coming off her, too bright to look at." Casey sat next to Lou in the bleachers by the ball field and asked, "What do you think?"

"Acid flashback?"

"Thanks. Why do I bother talking to you?"

"I don't know."

"After the dream, for a couple of hours, I felt great. I know I'll follow her into that big light."

"Since when do you believe in a big light?"

"That's Hospice speak." Casey finally smiled. "People always go into the light, never the dark."

"That would be too depressing."

Casey laughed. A couple of sea gulls flew over the ball field, looking for scraps of food.

"They don't know baseball season hasn't started yet," Lou said.

"Hope springs eternal. In the groups, they say, 'Oh you must have something you have to do first, before you die.' That's bullshit. I'm here because my heart is still beating. I get up, I eat. I'll let you know if I find some deeper purpose."

"I'm on the edge of my seat." Lou looked across the field and into the little redwood grove.

"I get some exercise, go to meetings. Lily died. I miss her every day, but she wouldn't want me to be morose. Well, I've said that before."

Lou drank some of his coffee. "I need a new dream too."

"Oh, this is about you now?"

"Me and my nightmare. Can't sleep for shit."

"The sky isn't going to open and show a long-bearded old geezer holding a thunderbolt and giving you the answer."

"I thought you were him."

"No beard, man. Look at me." Casey laughed. "What do I know?"

Lou watched the sea gulls fighting over a food wrapper. They knew what their purpose was. He felt a little jealous. Casey was quiet a while. A small child with a plastic baseball bat chased the sea gulls while his father trailed behind.

"You get to a point. Your life doesn't look good without your partner. I suppose you never felt that?"

"With Julie, for a while. Then it ended."

"You make that fateful decision. You stay. A few years go by, a decade. Suddenly, it's a whole life." Casey's voice trailed off, then he rallied. "Folks like you just don't get it. The modern world. Always something new. What if you can't get the one thing you want?"

"Which is?"

"That's up to you, Lou. Maybe the great adventure isn't another town in Northern California where you can be a handyman and a frustrated artist. April isn't going to be a friend with benefits for the next thirty years. You can take that to the bank. I know it still shocks you, but you have a kid."

The sea gulls were lifting off into the twilight now.

"Maybe you are the geezer god I was looking for," Lou said.

Casey said, "Something is leaving me, some big, dark cloud. I'm here now. The rest of my life is starting."

"For a moment there, I thought you were still grieving."

"My moods, they change so fast."

"Mine too," Lou said, finishing off his coffee. "Jennie's waiting on dinner."

"That's what I'm talking about," Casey said.

The boy ran after the gulls with his plastic bat, swinging at the sky, as if the rising moon were a distant piñata.

His father laughed and said, "Jackson, let's go home now and see Mommy."

Chapter 28

Lou Helps Yarrow Build the Set

"It's bitchin'. I got the part. The Fire Girl. My lines smoke, so to speak," Jennie said. She passed a bowl of soup to April.

"Typecasting, yeah," Lou said. "Where's Yarrow?"

"Working late at school," April said.

"Tech crew," Jennie said. "He's over his head."

"What's that supposed to mean?" April asked sharply.

"You'll see."

Lou served dinner out on his deck. The whispering sound the creek made brightened his mood.

"It's a remake of the Inferno," April said.

"The Fire Girl?" Lou asked.

"Okay, she was written into it by the drama teacher. I have to remember like so many lines. In the underworld, I scare Dante and Virgil. I tell them the truth. I'm so typecast. That's right, Dad. Perpetually PMS. I'm dyeing another red streak in my hair. I'm a method actor. Everything around me turns to fire. Be careful."

Suddenly, Jennie jumped up and started yelling and waving her hands, "You've come to the Inferno, and everything here burns up and dies, except me, ME!"

"Wow, great. Now eat your soup," Lou said.

"Jen, I'm proud of you," April said. "It's a great role."

"You're not my mother."

An awkward silence descended on the table.

"Ah, that didn't come out right," Jennie said.

"Jen, show some goddamn respect or go inside and finish your supper alone," Lou said.

"Okay, I'm sorry. It's my character who said that, not me."

"It's okay," April said. "Tell us some more about the play."

"Dress rehearsal is tomorrow night, then we do it Friday and Saturday. The drama teacher's husband, who's an architect, designed a mega-intense set. It's supposed to be done tonight."

"Theater is like that," April said.

"You gotta come," Jennie said to April.

"Me?" April asked.

"Yeah, that was kind of another apology."

"Okay," April replied.

Jennie's phone rang and she looked at Lou. "It's Yarrow. Can I?"

"Okay. Take it inside, please."

"Ah, Lou…"

"I know. I shouldn't have yelled at her."

"No. Thanks for the support." April put her hand on his. For a moment, the creek's whisper filled the space between them. "Step-parenting is a bitch."

"Tell me about it."

April and Lou heard Jennie's voice. "How should I know where the tech geeks are?" Then she came outside. "Yarrow's freaked out. Half the kids never showed up."

"I'll call him," April said.

"Yarrow is so high-drama," Jennie said.

Lou looked at her and raised his eyebrow.

"I am not."

After a short call, April came in. "Lou, will you talk to him?"

"What?" Lou was tired.

A few minutes later, he was loading his truck with his carpentry tools.

April was standing next to him. "Thanks, Lou," she said. She handed him a toolbox.

"Do you want to stay here with Jen?"

"I'll talk to her."

Yarrow was backstage at the high school when Lou found him.

"I was all excited about Tech Crew after you showed me some stuff with tools. Now look."

"What?"

"Well, I can't figure out the set. The kids who were going to help me bailed. The architect hasn't come yet."

"Okay. Okay. Show me the set."

"You're standing in it."

The floor was littered with old doors and windows, tall

papier-mâché columns, and stacks of curtains.

Lou followed Yarrow to the front of the big stage. Oddly shaped pieces of plywood were stacked haphazardly next to buckets of hinges and angle irons. Baskets of nails. Some tools were scattered around on the floor, drills and lengths of contractor-strength extension cord.

"This is a mess."

"Tell me about it. We're supposed to build stairs that are visible to the audience, and invisible stairs under trap doors. I have no clue."

"What's that?"

"It's a flame and smoke machine. The drama teacher wanted a real Inferno. This is going to be the worst day of my life. Tomorrow, when everyone troops in for dress rehearsal and I'm standing here with my thumb up my ass, going, 'Ah, ah.'"

"Yarrow, listen to me. My dad was an asshole but he taught me one important thing. Keep your head down and do the next thing."

"What?"

Lou assigned Yarrow to a simple task, cutting plywood into rectangles using a saber saw. He went to work on the hinged trap doors and steps.

By midnight, things were moving along. Lou was cutting a riser for the stairs when a tall man appeared.

"Oh, thank god. It's Mr. Thomas."

"Bill," he said to Lou as they shook hands. "Glad you're here. My job ran late. Then our daughter…"

"I know how that can go."

"We can do this, the three of us," Bill said. He strapped on his construction belt.

About four a.m., Yarrow hit himself on the finger three times with a hammer and yelled.

Lou said, "Okay, Yarrow, you go get some rest. Bill and I can…"

"No, I'm staying till the end."

"Tomorrow's a school day. Just go rest for a moment."

Yarrow went into a corner and lay down with a tarp over him.

At five, Bill said, "Damn, we're a couple of hinges short. I can't stay past eight."

"I have some at my shop."

"Good, I'll keep cutting up this plywood."

Lou and Bill reworked the hinges he'd brought from his shop, and then fit them onto the trap doors.

At six thirty, the men were finished. Lou woke up Yarrow. "Okay Yarrow, you can help us clean up."

He drove into the Orchard at about seven thirty and found April opening her car door.

"You stayed."

"We talked till too late."

"How's the couch?"

"I slept in the double bed with Jennie. Where's Yarrow?"

"Doing his homework at school. We finished."

"He'll be wrecked."

"He's fifteen."

"I've got to run home and change." She turned back to him. "Thanks, Lou. His dad never did shit for him."

"He did a good job," Lou said. "You can be proud."

April teared up. "You gave him a chance."

She got in the car and drove away. Lou felt the tug of family in his heart. He thought for a moment about the early days in Paradise, the farm, him and Jennie in the woods together.

He heard a crash in the cottage. Jennie yelled, "Goddamn it, dad. There's no milk."

Chapter 29

Angela's Office

"We all agree with the mother that this will be a starter office. A few small rooms and a larger meeting area. What do you think?" A young, energetic woman named Tessa showed Lou around the old store. Her long, curly, blond hair danced as she rolled her head back and forth.

"Mother?"

"Angela. My teacher. The owner."

"I usually like to meet with the owner."

"She doesn't see many people like you."

"Okay. You know, the last store was a marijuana front," Lou said.

"Mother erases all negative karma."

"Comforting," Lou said, looking around. "This building needs a lot of work."

April called this stretch of Bingo's commercial area, "the Bingo Triangle." Businesses moved in, then disappeared. The previous renters had destroyed the wooden shelves lining the walls, which had held hand-dripped candles and smoking paraphernalia. The floor was covered with dirt, sawdust, and boards with nails sticking out of them.

"With the number of people Angela's attracting, this will work for only a while. Then we'll move."

"Was she a volunteer for Hospice?"

"Angela? I doubt it. She has a higher calling."

Lou kicked aside some broken boards as he walked. "Do you have plans?"

"Are you coming on to me?" Tessa asked with a smile.

"No. Drawings for the job. Architecture."

"Oh, Angela can do all that. She's amazing. Money is coming, it's just not here yet. You know, 'do what you love.' Angela proves it to me every day. You can do it, right?" Tessa asked. "It's a rush job. Angela says we need security, a safe place for our sacred work."

"Mom needs a home."

"You got it. I was a massage therapist here in Bingo before I met the Angel, and now I just want to serve her. I have a sense of mission that I've never felt before."

I need that, Lou thought. But he wouldn't say it to Tessa. Something about her mercurial enthusiasm bothered him.

"We were hoping for a non-profit rate, if you have one," Tessa said. They were standing in the wall-less bathroom. "New fixtures, new sheet rock, etc."

"Lots of etcetera," Lou said. "I can work up an estimate if I have plans. BTW, all my work is non-profit."

"That's funny," Tessa said, taking his arm and guiding him towards the front of the building. The front door opened.

"Oh my god, here she is," Tessa said.

"In the flesh," Lou said. He had never seen Angela before. She walked in and doffed her strange hat.

"Mother," Tessa said. She quickly crossed the room, kissed the floor in front of Angela, and then hugged her.

Lou wondered what Central American tribe the hat was from. Strands of gray cotton were piled up and rolled around long, possibly illegal feathers.

"Mother, Mother, Mother," Tessa said.

"Yes, child."

"Here's the contractor we found."

"I'm Lou," he said, moving across the floor.

"Senor Lou, it's … how you say … a pleasure to meet you." Angela wouldn't let go of Lou's hand. When she looked him in the eye, he got a tremendous feeling of presence.

"Same here. With my knees, I won't kiss the floor."

"I feel your appreciation anyway. Your daughter's leg, it is healthy, ahora?"

"Yes. Uh, how did you know…"

"Mother knows everything," Tessa interrupted. The three of them stood in the middle of the room.

"Not quite, senorita."

"Thanks for helping her. She was pretty shook up when she fell."

"Si. We help, we build, we die. The end times are near, can

you feel? We all need full strength. That is why I have come. We'll build this little office, then a bigger one, then we all die together."

"Okay. So why build an office?" Lou asked. Angela's face shined, and Lou noted that her mouth was full of metal teeth. This wasn't his usual client interview.

"Senor, you feed your daughter knowing that she will die. Why shouldn't we pray with each other, have holy ceremonies until the last great moment?"

"You got me there," Lou said. His mind raced with thoughts but in his body he felt a strange warmth: Angela's transmission. He was drawn to her yet at the same time he resisted her predictions of doom.

"Yes, yes," Tessa said. Lou thought she was going to throw herself at Angela's feet again.

"What were you doing before you became a prophet?"

"Prophet? Like the Old Testament? Do you judge me, senor? I was tortured in Guatemala. An exquisite pain. I woke up to the truth of the Future. Now I tell it to people in Bingo who welcome me. How did I get here? I don't know. God found me a new home. My old one..." She started to weep copiously and tremble.

"Yes, we welcome you here," Tessa said. "Please, Mother, please."

Lou felt waves of her terror and loss move through him. Angela shuddered, then went on, as if nothing had happened.

"Senor Lou, what do you believe in?"

"Besides feeding my daughter?"

"You believe in beauty. I can see it in your hands."

"Okay." Again he thought, *How does she know?*

"And you know Beauty comes from the other world, no?"

"I know it comes from nature."

"And nature is infinito. Where does it stop? Everything in nature is born and dies. It is claro. You have account at the lumber store, yes?"

"Uh, sure."

"I need your help."

Lou surprised himself. "Yeah, sure."

"Gracias, senor. You will be repaid in Karma."

"Ah, Mother. I need cash."

"I must go ahora. Tessa will help you."

Everything about the job troubled Lou. It was too big for him and it would take too long. Every day he seemed more rooted in Bingo, but his nightmare got worse and worse. He was so tired of not sleeping. And now he was fronting money at the hardware store?

"Angela, wait a minute. My friend Casey said you worked for Hospice, then disappeared."

"I know no Casey. Maybe."

"Okay. Maybe someone else. We have a deal, as long as you cover the hardware store."

Angela took his hand and, again, he felt a jolt of energy in his body; not unpleasant, almost magnetic.

"I can deliver the plans to you soon," Tessa said, walking Lou towards a little table. "Do you have a contract?"

"Sure."

Lou turned to say goodbye to Angela, but she had left the room.

Chapter 30

Temptation

"Organic frozen pizza," Jennie yelled. "You're kidding me. Vitamins get killed nine different ways."

Lou put the warm pizza box down on the table. He wasn't having any of Jennie's food trips after a day spent tearing out one of Johnie's rotten decks.

"Can you cook?"

"Mom didn't teach me shit. And if I did cook, then I won't have time to study. I'd flunk math and become a tattooed barista."

"That's your shitty future," Lou said. He stood up from his seat at the table. "I've had it with your lack of gratitude."

He picked up the pizza box, walked over to the back door, and tossed it over the deck out into the back yard.

"Here's ten bucks. Go downtown and find something to eat. I don't want to look at you."

"Dad, now..."

"Go."

After Jennie left, Lou went out in the yard and gathered up the pizza slices. He wiped off the grass and dampness, then sat on his deck, eating peacefully.

"Are we done with that now?" Jennie said when she returned. Lou stopped doing dishes.

"Okay, I over-reacted," he said. "You too."

"I did not."

"Sit down with me for a minute."

Jennie noticed the empty box. "You ate the pizza?"

"Moving on. Terry and Kathy are coming to visit tomorrow."

"With Francesca?"

"Yes. They want to see where we live and say hello."

"They can't have my room."

"Yes, they can. You get the floor or you can sleep in the truck."

"Terry always wants something."

When did she become so perceptive? Lou wondered.

As soon as Terry, Kathy, and Francesca, Jennie's best friend forever, arrived, they all trooped out to the beach.

"Nice to see them together," Kathy said, as the two girls bounced arm in arm down the beach, talking furiously.

For a moment, for Lou, time dropped away. The two girls were five, splashing in the river by their little house in Paradise. He felt a weird warm feeling in his heart.

"Someone walked over your grave," Kathy said.

"Kids and water. So many memories. When I was a kid, we camped up on the Trinity with the Indians. Rope swings, hot dogs over the fire."

"So, your old man was nice to you," Terry said. He lay on his back, enjoying the sun.

"Once."

"Sometimes I look at your empty cabin from our porch and feel sad," Kathy said. "Other times, I think people like Julie are so ethereal, so spiritual that they can't stay long on earth."

"The drugs didn't help," Terry cut in.

"Lou, it's time for someone to live in your cabin," Kathy added. "Leaves pile up on the deck…"

Lou laughed and interrupted. "You want me there to sweep."

"No, sometimes I want someone living that close, someone like you," she said.

Terry stood up from the wide blanket, tied his graying hair into a ponytail, and took off his tee shirt. *After twenty-five years*, Lou thought, *he's still rail-thin, with webs of muscles in his long arms.* There was a sharpness in Terry's long, thin face and dark eyebrows, a tension in his lean form. Terry got what he wanted.

"We have a job for you. I'm putting some cash into solar, and I need a smart guy who knows electrical. I can guarantee you two years. That's longer than…"

He stopped when he saw Lou looking down the beach at his daughter splashing in the waves with Francesca.

"Jennie has friends. She has us," Kathy said. "We'd be a family again."

Lou threw small clots of sand towards the two sea gulls that were eyeing his lunch bag.

A family, Lou thought.

Terry continued, "I need someone I can trust."

"I'll think about it." Lou covered his face with his baseball hat and relaxed deeper into the sand.

"Look, it's America. My dad drove a truck. Now look at me, at us," Terry said. "We've had this conversation for fifteen years. You always wanted green living. Right?"

"You're a pot farmer with a shotgun by the front door."

"Lou, buddy. You want green. Try this." Terry took a roll of bills out of his shorts pocket. Hundreds, tied together with a rubber band. "This is fucking green. I'm giving you a chance to send Jennie to college."

"Unless your artwork starts to sell," Kathy added.

Jennie and Francesca were walking up and down on the beach, waving a cell phone in the air. They came over to the adults.

"Can't show Jennie that video of Tommie. Reception comes and goes."

"Tommie," Terry said.

"Dad."

"Oh crap, look who's coming over the hill," Jennie said.

April and Yarrow walked down the trail, carrying several brightly colored bags.

"Who's the stud muffin?" Francesca asked.

"His mom's stalking my dad."

"I asked them to join us," Lou said. "April and I are way past the stalking phase. Jennie forgets."

Jennie jumped in. "They're almost living together and pushing me out."

"I'm sure your dad will save a room for you." Kathy laughed.

"I want to meet him," Francesca said standing up and brushing sand off her red bikini.

"Sit down. Oh god, they saw us."

"Come on." Francesca pulled Jennie up and they intercepted the arriving twosome. April nodded after a moment, and Yarrow dropped his three bags and an umbrella. The three teens plunged into the bay, yelling and splashing.

After April joined the adults, Kathy asked, "How did you meet Lou?"

"He fixed my plumbing."

Terry snorted.

Lou always felt embarrassed when people talked about him as if he weren't there. *Do any of these people know me?* he asked himself.

Francesca did a few quick flips off the raft. Then Yarrow landed on his stomach while trying one. Lou could see the pink flush on his chest when he climbed back on the raft. Francesca pushed Jennie into the water. The teens sunned themselves for a few minutes, then rolled back and forth in a big pile.

They swam back to the beach and ran up towards their towels. Yarrow had filled in a little. His brain and body seemed to be communicating better.

"Dad," Francesca began. "Yarrow touched me. You know. Touched me."

Terry stood up and turned towards Yarrow. "What? Where?" Lou had seen that violent posture many times.

"No. No, sir. They grabbed me." Yarrow flushed red. "No."

Jennie burst out laughing, then Francesca.

Francesca said, "She told me to say that."

Chapter 31

More Temptation

"When are you going to that deck done?" Johnie yelled from his big Chevy pick up truck. Lou and Terry drank coffee and stood by Terry's big four-wheeler, where they were loading duffel bags.

Lou raised his coffee cup in salute and said nothing, as Johnie roared off.

A subtle, warm breeze blew up the creek bed. Lou still felt content. He didn't have to go anywhere. He had work after his friends left. The girls were finishing breakfast inside.

"I'm guessing that prick is your landlord?" Terry said. "I'd never talk to you like that."

"Remember the day I was leaving Paradise?"

"That doesn't count."

"I thought about what you said yesterday, Terry. In the night, when I couldn't sleep. I'm not saying yes. There has to be a firewall between the solar company and..."

"I know. I'll have an accountant."

"I can't live on the property."

"That's part of your salary."

"No. It's too close to the pot grow. Plus Jennie."

"Okay. You find a cabin or something. "

"One more thing."

"Okay."

"Don't get fucking caught."

Terry turned towards him with a look in his eye that Lou had seen before, like at the beach at Shelter Cove, when they had been looking at some hellacious waves. Terry never made the long drive without surfing. He always said, "Come on, man. It's just a wave."

When you looked down off a North coast winter wave, you saw more than water. You saw your life pass before your eyes. And you went out, into the grey-green churning mass, because

Terry went.

He raised his coffee cup and clinked it with Lou's. "That's the plan, answer man."

Back inside, the girls were playing cards with Kathy and April.

"Uno, bitch," Jennie yelled.

Francesca yelled, "No, no."

"We gotta go, girls," Kathy said. "Jennie, draw four."

"No," Jennie protested. "Can we finish? Come on."

Kathy smiled at Terry and they both nodded. They could wait half an hour.

After the loaded truck had left the driveway, Lou and Jennie were alone, finishing the dishes.

"It's so psycho," Jennie said. "Terry is the serpent."

"What?"

"He looks like a snake. In my mythology class, the Garden of Evil."

"Eden."

"Whatever. Terry tempts you. You're the innocent Adam. It's perfect. According to the wing nuts in Humboldt, marijuana bushes are the tree of the knowledge of good and evil," Jennie said.

"You were eavesdropping."

"It's my life, too. I told you Terry…"

"You were right."

Lou looked around. They lived in a shabby cabin with secondhand furniture. Jennie had added colorful pillows and drapes, but the dingy feeling was still there.

"Would it be so bad?"

"I can't go back." She fell silent.

"Now you like it here. Yesterday you hated it."

"My hormones are swinging. Satan offers Adam and Eve the apple. They fall for it. I can't go back to Paradise. I'm telling you, and that's exactly what God told Adam."

"You can't go back because of the Bible?"

"It's not just a story, Dad. It's how we organize our lives."

"Around the Old Testament? I'll finish that pan."

"I finally get what Mrs. Dal means. She speaks English, with an English accent. That's so weird. She's right. We can't go back."

"Because of what happened to Adam?"

"Dead on, dude. Terry is the serpent. Besides, you're dating April. What would she say?"

"I'm not 'dating' April." Lou used air quotes.

"What are you doing?"

Chapter 32

Lou, Jennie and His Gun

"There's food in the refrigerator," Lou said when Jennie got home from school.

"Yeah." She sat down in the little living room without looking at him. That was fine with Lou. He concentrated on his bills, many of which were overdue.

After a while, adding up figures, it all made sense to Lou. He worked and people paid him. A basic human exchange. A fair day's wage. He could afford Jennie's constant assault on the food supplies, he had new wood for carving, and his truck ran.

He took a deep breath and put a hand on the pile of papers as a warm wind drifted up the creek and ruffled his pile of invoices.

Jennie punched away on her phone for a half an hour, and then asked, "Is there anything to eat, Dad?"

Lou waited a beat and said, "In the refrigerator."

"Did you say that already? Why is reception so crappy here?"

Every few minutes, Jennie shook her phone or tapped it on the coffee table in front of her snack.

"Does that help?" Lou asked, finding the noise and movement distracting.

"Goddamn it," she said.

"What? Language." Lou lifted his head from his list of figures.

"That asshole Luke. He's following me around."

"Jennie, boys stare at you because you're beautiful. We've talked about…"

"No, he was on campus, making weird hand gestures, like, you know, whacking off, and trying to get my attention. Now he sends me a picture and wants to be friends."

Lou got a weird, cold feeling. "Let me see."

"No. It's my phone."

"Jennie, give me the phone."

Luke's thin, sardonic face smiled at Jennie from the Facebook page.

"These stupid gang gestures," Lou said. "How did he get your number?"

"It's Facebook, Dad. You can 'friend' anyone."

Jennie started her homework. Lou stared at his hardware store bills for a few moments, then he went over to Luke's cabin.

Luke was rubbing his eyes when he opened the door.

"What do you do besides sleep?"

"None of your fucking business."

"Stalking my daughter is my business."

"She's not yours. She's grown up. She's mine now. You'll see."

"Stay away from her."

"It's a mean world, man. She wants to go to Oregon with me. That's what she told me. She hates Bingo. She hates you, too."

"Did you hear me say, 'stay away'?"

"Get off my porch. Harder men than you don't scare me."

Lou went home and took a locked metal box from under his bed. He sat down with Jennie in the living room and showed her a pistol.

"Holy shit. I didn't know..."

"Since Paradise. Terry gave it to me."

"To protect the fields."

"Did you ever shoot one?"

"Some of the boys had air rifles. I could hit..."

"This is no air rifle."

"Did you ever use it?"

Lou was silent for a few moments.

"On some bottles.

"Dad."

"Here's how it works."

He showed her where the safety was and how to load it. "And here's the combination to the lock box. It's under my bed."

Lou was out late working the next evening, trying to seal a water leak, when his cell phone rang. Jennie.

"Dad, he's here. "

In the background, Lou heard another voice.

"He came inside the house. He says he is fixing the plumbing. He won't leave."

"Put him on."

"He thinks we're moving to Oregon."

"I'm on my way." Lou dropped his tools where he was working and ran for the truck.

When he got home, the front door had three bullet holes in it.

"Sorry about the door, Dad. If I had wanted to hit him, I would have."

Chapter 33

Angela's Attraction Grows

"People were standing in the street listening to a loudspeaker when I went by Angela's office last night," April said. "Can't help that."

"She's hit this town like wildfire."

"Is that the image you want?" Jennie asked. "You know, with the drought?"

Lou cringed a little at Jennie's outspokenness. The awkward foursome, April, Lou, Jennie and Yarrow, was eating soup at April's apartment.

"Probably not," April said. "I'll clean up my analogies."

"You're the one who's had fire on the brain since the play," said Yarrow, who was looking at his left hand in his lap. Lou didn't think he was listening.

"Drop dead," Jennie said. "I didn't pick the Inferno. Summer school is okay. We're onto Myths of Fire and Water."

"Yeah, the biblical flood at your house." Yarrow kept the pressure on. "You forgot the ark."

"That's what Mrs. Dal said, not me, moron."

"Hey," April said. She served more soup.

"I have no idea what Angela says to adults," Jennie added. "She still meets with us at the park."

"Do you want me to hear her talk, Jennie?" Lou asked.

"I can't believe I'm hearing this from you, the skeptic," April said.

"I'm trying to support my daughter's spiritual and mythic growth."

"For once," Jennie said.

"Shit, Jennie, you must be PMS," Yarrow said. She gave him the finger.

"Apparently, people are starting to give Angela donations, so that she can buy some property," April continued. "I heard it at the hair salon."

"Dad, you could donate all your carved rats to help her. Then they'd never scare me again."

"I want the coyotes," April laughed.

"That's your old man's retirement plan, Jen. Do you want to support me?"

"No problem. I'll become famous, Jenni-fire, a one-name celebrity."

"You still better go to college," April said.

Lou gave her a look.

"Uh-oh," April said.

"I almost said, 'You're not my mother,' but I didn't." Jennie laughed. "I must be starting to like you."

Yarrow looked up from his phone, "She's not a pet, Jennie."

"Shut up and eat," replied Jennie.

Four spoons found their way to four mouths. "Good soup," Lou said.

"Angela's the best thing to happen to Bingo since the vegan restaurant," Jennie said. "I plan on working there if I stay around here."

"The restaurant closed this week," Lou said.

"The food was horrible," Yarrow said. "They should have cooked some of it."

"Who else besides Angela is inspiring the kids of Bingo?" Jennie asked.

"Transgendered Hollywood celebrities?" Yarrow asked. He waved his phone. "Look, I don't care what these bozos do at home but I don't want to know about it."

"Don't look," April said. "We're having dinner."

"It's the end time: fire and brimstone," Jennie said.

"So says Angela, the prophet." Yarrow laughed. "It's such bullshit."

"Language," Lou and April said at the same time.

"What do you think, Yarrow?" April asked.

"It's the end time for me if I don't get my bike fixed. Team tryouts start in a few weeks."

"I'll look at it with you," Lou said.

"Yarrow, no phones at dinner, I told you."

"You wanted me to take summer school. I'm doing my homework."

"Right," Jennie scoffed. She leaned over and looked towards his phone. "Transgender fashions?"

"No, I dropped that one. It's my class, Journalism on the Web."

"No one's inspiring the adults of Bingo, either," April continued.

"I know why the kids like to hear it," Jennie said. "Maybe it's nice to hear an adult take the end of life on earth seriously."

"It's nice?" April asked.

"Yeah. That's what it feels like around here sometimes," Yarrow said.

"That's her attraction?" Lou replied. "All of us dead?"

"Dad, she didn't invent the end time, you know. Like, I can't tell if she's talking about letting go of negative, constrictive thoughts or about the whole planet going up in a ball of nuclear flames. Her talks are more poetry than logic."

Lou thought, *My daughter is smarter than* me.

A couple of nights later, Jennie, Lou and April walked into town for Angela's Friday night talk.

"You did a nice job, Lou," April said, admiring the glassed-in cabinets in the foyer. Soft trance music played in the background, and incense sticks burned in front of two tall Buddha statues.

"I better take off my deodorant," Lou said, as he read through the list of instructions about the event.

"Your manly smell will paralyze sensitive women," April said.

"Story of my life."

"Your shoes, sir," said one of the white-clad attendants.

About sixty people sat close together in the meeting room, on pillows and chairs in rows. An excited murmur filled the room. A thin woman in a long, plain, white dress was finishing up a detailed talk. "Then when she arrives, we stand and bow. Oh gosh, that's her now."

Lou looked out a wide window he had installed. A large black Mercedes sedan was pulling across a parking lot covered in gravel. The crunching sound filled the room. An air of expectancy replaced the sound of the students chatting.

After the talk, Lou, Jennie and April stopped at the organic ice cream shop in downtown Bingo.

"She's a powerful presence, don't you think, Lou?" April asked.

"He fell asleep," Jennie said.

"I'm still hungry," Lou said, swiping the inside of his tiny bowl with his tongue.

"Dad, that's gross. If my friends..."

"Jennie, what did you think?" April interrupted.

"You don't want me to correct my father? That's cool. Well, the whole entrance thing is beautifully staged. Then the talk, with a devotional close for the suckers."

"Close?" April asked.

"'Close the deal.' Salesman slang. I learned it in my business class."

"The whole bells-and-whistles show is one big manipulation of feeling," April said. "Angela says 'Listen to me carefully now because you might not get another chance. And you better change your ways.' I caught myself nodding along."

"I felt that," Lou said. "I caught myself reaching for my wallet."

"After you woke up," Jennie interjected.

"Then I realized I'd have to save some money for ice cream. Like, two hundred dollars. Please don't tell me you want more."

"If the end is near, why does she need four million dollars?" April asked.

Lou choked on his glass of water. "I love it when you're cynical. Takes the pressure off me."

"Oh, I can go dark, Lou. Believe me. And the way she talked to her students when they asked questions, at least tonight. Jesus. It's a wonder anyone asks about anything. She seems so impatient."

"Maybe the end is very near and she's pressed for time." He laughed. "I don't know anyone who repeats their problems endlessly, do you?"

"Are you talking about me?" April asked.

"Are you talking about me?" Jennie asked. "I can't help it if I feel like Luke always in the woods, staring at me."

"I haven't seen him this week."

"I've been keeping an eye out for him at school," April said.

"You know what they say about Germans, don't you?" Lou asked.

"She's Guatemalan."

"A German is either at your throat or at your feet."

"So why are we talking about Germans?" April asked. "What's the connection?"

"All the Nazis went to Guatemala," Jennie interjected. "Everyone knows that."

"Argentina," April said. "Germans? Why are we…"

"Some people feel good only when they're either dominating or being dominated," Lou said.

"Luke wants to dominate me," Jennie said.

"That can be fun," April said, licking her spoon.

"April, please," Jennie protested. "That's gross."

"I'm not laughing about Luke," Lou said.

Chapter 34

Luke's Chemistry Experiment

"What's that horrible smell?" Jennie asked Lou.

They were walking one Friday evening in the hills. Redwood needles crunched under their feet. Lou loved the evening quiet, when the town had settled down. The low hum of traffic noise had dropped to almost nothing.

Tomorrow, he could relax on his deck, or maybe in his shop, where a redwood-and-oak bald eagle waited for him, half-done. Money would take care of itself. A large rabbit hopped across their path.

"Oh shit. I should have known," Lou said, looking down into the Orchard property and towards Luke's rundown cottage

"What? I saw a light down there late one night." Lou noticed how observant Jennie was.

"It's a meth lab."

"Let's go see."

"No. I heard one blow up once."

"In Paradise?"

"No. I should have known. Luke has been looking worse and worse all summer. I keep thinking he's gone away for good, but he's always back."

"I didn't shoot him yet," Jennie said.

"You're practicing restraint," Lou said.

"He asked me if I knew any chemistry."

"You talked to him."

"I can't help it if he follows me. I thought he was dealing pot, with all those cars coming here."

"Let's go back. I have to go talk to Johnie."

"Okay. I have homework."

When Lou walked up on his deck, Johnie put down his beer bottle, next to three empties on a worn wicker table.

"Lou, my brother," he said. "Do you want one?"

"Fuck, are you drunk? We got to talk."

137

"You're goddamned intimidating. Sit down next to me."

"Do you know what Luke is doing?"

"Fixing the plumbing in your house?" Johnie gave a sullen laugh.

"That's not funny."

"I don't want to know."

"He's making meth."

"So?" Johnie pulled the tab on another beer and tossed his empty towards the creek.

"I can't be anywhere around that shit."

"I knew you never commit to an actual job."

"This conversation is about a meth lab, Johnie."

"We all have family to take care of, don't we?"

"You can't keep this a secret. You can lose your property. Plus the fire danger."

"You think I haven't thought of all this, asshole?"

Johnie finished his beer and tossed it into the yard, towards the family cemetery.

"For god's sake, Lou. Quit pacing and sit down. Nothing's going to happen tonight."

Towards the back of the property, they heard the sound of a rough car engine and then car doors.

"I appreciate your concern, Lou. I really do." Johnie looked blank for a few moments. Then he pointed down at the row of tombstones. "You can't make me feel worse, Lou. It's them I answer to. And I let them down."

"What?"

"Luke was part of the last loan. The last. I had to give him a 'job.'" Johnie made air quotes. "I finally lost my father's legacy. I'm just the manager now. Have a beer with me?"

Lou turned to leave. Then they heard the sharp crack of an explosion. A flash of light filled the sky.

"It's the lab," Lou said. "Call 911."

Chapter 35

Yarrow Erupts

After Lou and April cleaned up the dinner dishes, April dealt the Uno cards. April's little apartment felt warm and intimate, with Jennie there.

"Yarrow's at mountain bike practice," Lou noted.

"He's never home with us," April said.

"Us?" Jennie asked. She picked up her cards and sorted them.

"Working on your pronouns?" Lou asked.

"I'm getting used to it," April responded. "Us."

"Yeah," Jennie said and rearranged her cards.

"Uno," Jennie yelled about fifteen minutes later. April groaned.

Lou looked over his fourteen cards. Did he have a 'Draw four' card to give her? Yes. He laid it down.

"No, I can't believe you're my father." Jennie refilled her hand with cards.

"Did I complain when you gave me one ten minutes ago?"

"Guys don't complain..." Jennie said.

"You're learning about gender roles." April laughed.

"Guys don't complain," Jennie continued. "They stalk."

"Are you still worrying about Luke?" April asked.

"Yeah. I never knew how vulnerable a girl could feel."

"Goddamn it," Lou said. April took out a card and laid it on the pile.

Jennie put down her last card a few minutes later and yelled, "Victory!"

As April shuffled for the next game, Jennie asked her, "Hey, would you talk to me about college sometime? I get confused."

"What did you want to know?"

"Like, how do you figure out your major?"

Lou laughed.

"What?"

"I changed majors a few times before I dropped out," he said.

Were they becoming a family? Something warm started in his heart and spread around inside his body.

"Me too," April said.

"But everyone has their college major figured out."

"Jennie, listen to me," April said. "High achievers never sleep, they're so anxious. Do you want to be like that? Go to Europe, take a gap year and learn to play the flute."

"Really. I could go to this cool skateboard school in San Francisco and finish my GED there. Right, Dad?"

"Thanks, April." Lou laughed again. "I was thinking community college a little further north."

"You won't get a real job and send me to Stanford."

"Not to major in skateboards. Let's see," Lou said, ticking off points on his fingers. "Single parent, dead mother, first-generation college. You should qualify for some real cash. Maybe I should get disabled."

"Lou, stop it."

A large crash sounded as the front door opened.

"That's my boy," April said.

Jennie snickered.

"Yarrow, you could have called."

"I fell on my phone when my bike blew up."

Yarrow dragged his mud-splattered bike through the kitchen. A pedal hit the wall and made a big dent.

"Oh shit," he said.

"Oh shit is right," April said. "And look at the mud."

"You said you wanted me to ride."

"I can fix it," Lou said.

"Right," Yarrow said. "I thought you fixed my chain. I pushed this thing for the last hour."

"I patched the tire," Lou said, defending himself.

"Right."

Yarrow rolled his bike into his bedroom, showered quickly, and then sat down to eat soup.

"I went up to where the Guatemalan guru lady has the tent show," he said. "Up on the mountain."

"That's a long ride," Lou said.

"Yeah, made longer by..."

"I want to go up there," Jennie said. "And see the camp."

"Don't," Yarrow said. "Luke would ask you to go to Oregon."

"He's up there?"

"Shit," Lou said.

"Language, Dad."

"The police want to have a little chat with him," April said.

"I'm not ratting him out."

"I'll take care of that. And I can take another look at your bike," Lou said.

Yarrow put down his spoon and looked at Lou.

"That's your style, man. Take another look at it. You can't do anything right." Yarrow was shouting now. "What are you doing here? Look, I just want to ride my bike, and you can't even help with that. I pushed it three fucking miles."

"Yarrow," April said. "Calm down."

"I said I'd take another look at it." Lou wanted to blast Yarrow but thought better of it.

Yarrow paced the floor, tall and gawky, waving his arms. "You're not my stepfather. I never know when is the last time I'll see you. It wouldn't be soon enough. And now, goddamn it, you're not even my bike mechanic."

"That's enough, Yarrow," April said. She started to stand up from the table.

"No, let him speak," Lou said.

"Are you staying or going? My mother doesn't care. You should hear what she says when you're not here. Do you know how much pain…"

"That's enough, Yarrow," April said.

Lou looked at April.

"I can explain," she said.

Lou looked back at his cards. Yarrow snorted. He flung himself down onto a wooden kitchen chair and ate some soup. He checked his phone periodically and watched them play cards.

"Okay, deal me in," Yarrow asked.

A few rounds of cards later, April said, "Well, what was it like up there?"

"Where?"

"At the tent camp." April collected all the cards and started shuffling.

"We snuck in, me and Bernie."

"Bernie and I," April corrected.

"Whatever. We parked our bikes and walked in through the front gate. Some lady asked, 'Are you part of Angela's army?' I lied. 'Sure, we go to all her talks.' The lady grabs my arm. She wants to take me straight to the Mother. That freaked me out. I already have a mother."

"Thanks, Yarrow."

"I could trade you in, you know." Yarrow noted April's expression. "Only kidding. Anyway, Angela's in the middle of a long talk. You know, the end of this, the end of that. Same shi ... sorry. Then a couple of hours of entertainment. One lady fell during the fire walk. What a mess. Fire-eaters, fire jugglers, torches everywhere. Bernie and I had some super-hot Mexican tacos that got made by some of Angela's Spic ... I mean Mexican buddies."

"Yarrow."

"We see Luke tending a big bonfire. I mean, big. Fire rose over our heads. He and a bunch of Goth assholes are dancing around it like madmen, waving sticks and shouting slogans. Then Luke starts kicking at the flaming logs and scattering them around, swinging big burning limbs at his buddies.

"Luke sees me and comes running. He says, 'Jennie has to leave with me.' I say, 'It's fucking summer, dude. Put the fire out.' Bernie looks at me like 'Who's this dork?' and we take off. Oh, yeah. The mother with the weird hat comes out of the dark and gives me a note for you, Lou."

He handed Lou a torn, folded piece of paper.

"How did she know you knew me?"

"No clue."

The foursome played cards for a while. As Lou and Jennie left for their car, April said, "Lou, can you come back? I can explain."

"Maybe tomorrow."

Chapter 36

Lou Goes to Angela's Ranch

As he drove up the twisting roads and into the hills towards Angela's ranch, Lou's big hope for the meeting was that she would pay for the job he'd done at her office. The hardware store had called him twice, so he was angry.

The bright summer light bouncing off the redwood branches danced in a slight breeze and calmed him a little. He pulled the truck over to the side of the road to enjoy it, and the view across the hills towards the ocean.

As he drove up to a run-down ranch house at the end of the road, Lou saw several people emptying a U-Haul truck: five-gallon bottles of water; big bags of potatoes and rice; long, closed wooden boxes.

Angela met him on the wide porch.

"You bought the whole ranch," Lou said as they settled around a table on the deck. He wondered where the money had come from, as Angela poured tea.

"God provides, but we don't talk about that," Angela said. She wore a loose, embroidered cotton dress and a necklace with several long feathers hanging down.

"I thought you wanted me to do more work, no?"

"No, no mas tiempo for building ahora."

Lou drank his tea as half a dozen people brought boxes and bags past him, into the house. "Planning a big party?"

"You Americans want to know everything," Angela said. "There is no answer."

They finished their tea and Angela said, "Come inside."

In the kitchen, a large industrial stove was being installed amidst sheet rock dust and timbers from knocked-down walls.

"What's in the long boxes?"

"You know, Lou."

"Do your students know?"

"We're almost listo for…"

"The end times."

"It comes, senor."

They walked down a hall lined with fifty-pound bags of rice, to a quiet room at the back of the house.

"Meditationes. Do you, Lou?"

"What?"

They sat on pillows on the floor.

"You came to my class en la ciudad, no? I have a vision of you, healing you?"

"From what?"

"You must tell to me. Now we meditate and you will know. Will you stay an hour?"

Lou looked at his watch. He was still hopeful about the money.

"Always measuring el tiempo. There is an infinity of time."

"Even when the end is near, I have to work."

"But porque?"

"Jennie?"

"Yes, the daughter you must protect. You can't protect."

"I can try."

"Meditate with me ahora. Just close your eyes."

Lou sat quietly for several minutes. He heard Angela breathe deeply a few times.

"You want a healing, yes?" Angela said.

Lou thought for a moment. "Yes."

"Your dream," Angela said. "It is the healing." They both breathed together for a few minutes while Lou wondered what she meant. His eyes were closed. Then his nightmare started while he was awake. This waking dream had never happened to him before. He saw his father yelling at him. Then his old pickup started to burn and roll down a long hill into a lake. He ran after the truck and jumped into it.

He opened his eyes. Angela was looking at him. He was breathing hard. "Do not stop the meditation," she said.

Ripples of energy moved through his body, as if he were shivering. Then peace arose in his chest, and he stopped panting.

"What happens after you jump in the truck?" she asked.

"What?" Lou was groggy. "I don't know." How did she know about the truck?

"Use your imagination now," she said. "What happens in the dream?"

"I don't know. I drive away. I drive to Bingo."

'Yes," she said. "Now you can meditate some more." Lou's breathing returned to a normal pace, and he felt relaxed.

Finally, after an hour, a bell rang somewhere.

"Lou, you're brave. We are done now."

Lou was exhausted. So many thoughts. So many images. He felt worn down by his whole life, not just the meditation. He could barely lift his eyes. In the afternoon twilight, Angela had a weird glow around her.

"Mother, where should I go? What should I do?"

"Who are you, my son? That's what you want to know. Come sit by me now."

Lou barely had enough energy to crawl over to her.

She wrapped her arms around him. Lou smelled perfume and flowers. He relaxed in a way he'd never felt before. Like all the wires in his body had finally broken, and he could soften.

"You are better now, senor," she said. "I love you."

Lou had a vision of carving an image of Angela into a great redwood stump he'd collected, a large Madonna. He thought of April with great gratitude, a depth of feeling that surprised him.

Then he fell asleep.

When he woke up, Angela was gone. He felt calm. He had slept, and he not been awakened by his nightmare.

It was dark. He walked outside, towards his truck.

Tessa, Angela's assistant, set down the crate of orange juice she was unloading and came over to him. Sweat had plastered her blond curls to her forehead. "You look stoned, Lou."

"I feel goofy, it's true."

She took his arm. "Most people leave a donation after a session with the Mother. You had quite a healing."

"Everyone seems to think so, " Lou said. "Ah, you still owe me from the job."

Tessa laughed, "Oh brother. That's another world. You won't live long enough to spend that money."

"Will Angela live long enough to spend my donation?"

"At the burn rate around here." Tessa laughed again. "Oh yeah. I wish you'd call her Mother. She has been kinder to you than your own mother ever was."

"Really." Lou was getting his feet on the ground. He started to protest but couldn't find the energy.

He got in his truck and drove down the hill into Bingo. He couldn't find any anger inside himself about the money. In fact, he felt curiously calm.

Chapter 37

The Fire Training

" Jesus brings the cleansing fire this year," said a thin, grey-haired woman. She wore a faded "Jesus Saves" tee shirt. She put a couple of ratty cloth bags down on the seat next to her. "This town needs it bad."

"You're sure?" April asked.

"Jesus is coming. He's coming in fire and he's coming soon."

"So you came to the community preparedness meeting."

"I go where Jesus tells me." The woman looked at April for a moment. Then she sat down in a front-row seat, and started going through her bags and mumbling to herself.

Lou and April stood with Casey and a few friends from the Orchard, waiting for the meeting to start.

The grey-haired woman turned and looked at April. "My pastor said we spread the word of Jesus wherever we are, and here I am. You're not listening, are you?"

"I've got enough problems," April replied.

"What?" the woman asked. Lou looked at April and raised an eyebrow.

"Some shit you can't let pass," April said.

"I guess," he responded. Normally at a meeting like this, he would be tripping about how fire could sweep through his shop or threaten Jennie. But tonight, he felt curiously calm.

"Ladies and gentlemen, please sit down," a handsome man in a blue fireman's uniform said to the crowd of twenty people. When he raised his hand to push back his longish grey hair, it got tangled in the gold braid hanging off his shoulder. Four younger men in uniform stood around the room, their muscled forearms crossed.

"We're here for you," the fireman continued. "You asked us about evacuation routes..."

The grey-haired woman interrupted from the first row. "Who's going to help me get out? I don't have a car. How can..."

"Ma'am, we'll get to that."

"I wish she'd make up her mind," April whispered to Lou. "Does she want to be rescued or ascend directly to heaven?"

"Shh," Jennie said. "I'm doing research for my class."

"We'll review the different fire organizations that support you, the most fire-prone areas near here, and plans to get you out safely. These men standing around the room are trained to help you. They went to the Sierra fire and single-handedly saved fifty-one houses in a small town. Two of your local firemen were hospitalized with burns."

Applause broke out and the burly young men waved to the audience.

"This promises to be an intense fire season," the chief continued. "We're sure, due to current modeling, that Bingo will have a big fire in the next few years. It doesn't look good. We know this is going to happen soon. I can take some questions now."

"Jesus is lord. Make the way ready for him," shouted the lady in the front row.

April jumped up. "It might happen, right? Emphasis on the word 'might.' I have students at the high school who can't sleep nights now. They're so disturbed."

"Lady, I'll be honest with you. We need to motivate you, your neighbors, the government..."

"By scaring the shit out of us? You don't know for sure it'll happen," she insisted.

"This town needs a good fire," shouted someone in the back. "It's so boring."

"That can't be," Lou said.

"He waved at me," Jennie said.

"Oregon," Luke yelled. "We'll be safe in Oregon. Jennie?"

"Next question," the chief said.

"I saw the Dominican College fire, down in Marin," Johnie said. "The old redwood went up like a torch. I have cabins. Can you protect them?"

"We hope so."

"Fire, one of the four Horsemen of the Apocalypse," the woman yelled.

"Actually, not," said Jennie, standing. She looked at some

notes she had taken. "Everyone has seen a fire. It's in our DNA. Its story interests me, Prometheus stealing fire."

The chief looked puzzled. "It's no story, young lady. Not here, not now."

"But it hasn't happened. That makes it a fantasy."

"She's right," Luke yelled.

"Call it a model, a projection," the chief said. "It's what we do. Next question."

"I know what you mean, Jennie," April whispered. "Why scare the…"

"I get it," Jennie interrupted.

As the meeting broke up, Lou said, "Let's go, now."

But Luke blocked their path. "What you said was so cool, Jennie. It is a story. These dumbasses don't get it."

"Blowing up the lab and starting a fire was no story," April said to Luke.

"Who the fuck are you?" Luke asked.

"Get him out of here," Lou said to Johnie, who had walked up behind Luke.

"She's fucking going to Oregon with me," Luke yelled. "Not with you, bitch."

Johnie pulled on Luke's arm and they walked away.

April asked Lou, "Are you moving to Oregon now?"

"Hell no," Lou responded.

As Lou, April and Jennie walked through town, back to the Orchard, Jennie said, "And those guys know fire, wow. I felt high just listening to them talk about it. It's like fire is their friend, their lover."

"The Jesus lady and Luke think we need a fire," Lou said. "That boy is dangerous. The Bingo police…"

"Have mounted a massive manhunt," April said. "All three of them."

"I want to call them," Jennie said. She dialed, then she slapped her phone down in her other hand. "Of course, busy."

"Luke worries you," April said.

"He's a moron," Jennie said. "He's right about the town. No wonder we hang out at the strip mall."

"You're picking up city ways," Lou said.

"Shut up, Dad," Jennie said. "Bingo doesn't qualify as a city."

"You can stay home and polish your nails, if you don't have anything to do. As long as you stay away from Luke."

"Don't worry."

"I've got to leave the Orchard, or he does."

"You and your Tom Cruise imitation can always come over to my condo," April said.

"What about me?" Jennie asked.

April looked at Lou, who said nothing. He watched himself relax. Did he have to explain everything to Jennie? On a warm summer night, he could walk towards downtown with his family. Tomorrow's troubles could wait.

Jennie noticed his silence.

"Thanks, Dad. 'Put your head down and drive through the fire,' the chief said. 'Watch the white line in the middle of the road.' Great. There's no lines on the roads in our neighborhood."

"And you can't drive," Lou said. "Don't worry about it yet."

"I think we need an ice cream cone," April said as they passed through Bingo's tiny commercial district. "Something cold."

Chapter 38

The Fire

"I don't like this," Lou said. "I lost everything in a fire. The air felt just like this."

"Where was that?"

"I don't want to talk about it. I'm so tired."

"At least this morning you have a good reason." April laughed and leaned into him. They had gone back to bed after Jennie had left for town on a muggy summer weekend morning. A dry wind blew insistently up the creek bed. After a long stretch of dry days, August was turning into September. Lou and April were standing naked outside on his deck.

"The air feels warm on my skin."

"You feel good on my skin, but I don't like muggy, smoky. Jennie's downtown. Where's Yarrow?"

"Biking with Bernie and the team. I'm touched."

A fire truck, its siren howling, went by on Drake Boulevard, several blocks away.

"It's been smoky for three weeks," April said. "The Clear Lake fire."

"This is worse. Something's wrong."

She went into the house and brought out her phone. "Of course, nothing."

"I want to get Jennie. Coming?"

"Okay. First…"

"What?"

"We should probably get dressed. Hey, come here."

"What?"

"This is nice. I like you." She kissed him.

Drake's bumper-to-bumper traffic barely moved. The radio in the truck said that a fire was under control in the hills above the next town over.

"That's where the smoke is coming from," April noted.

Another fire truck plowed through the heavy traffic.

"We're one idiot away from gridlock," Lou said.

Lou spotted Jennie's bright red hair flowing over a curb at the Parkade, a large parking area in the middle of town. He made a quick U-turn, parked facing towards the Orchard, and walked towards a group of teens.

"Jennie."

"What?" She rolled through some parked cars and came towards Lou and April. "We're going to the skate park. We have a car. Please."

"Jennie, get in the fucking truck."

"Uh-oh. What did I do?"

"No, I'm scared."

"Of what?"

"Look around."

Two fire engines tore down Drake as traffic parted in front of them. Now both lanes of traffic were snarled. "Ah, where's the fucking truck?"

Lou pointed up the road. "Look, if everything's okay, I'll take you to the park myself. You can meet your friends in an hour or two."

"Shit."

"Language, language. That's two."

"Don't you lose a point for 'fucking truck'?"

"Do you know which way Yarrow went?" April asked, when Jennie and Lou returned to the truck.

"How should I know?" Jennie waved her arm at the mountain overlooking the town.

"Shit," April said. She took out her phone as they piled into the truck.

"It's been smoky for a month," Jennie said.

"Shit, no service now." April put her phone back in her pocket.

An hour later, April had walked out to the road four more times to try to reach Yarrow. The dry wind blew harder and harder. Lou put the two hand-carved coyotes and a half-finished eagle into his truck, with a set of expensive chisels, while Jennie watched.

"Uh, Dad."

"What?"

"At school we had like a drill. What about important papers, photos, cash?"

"Ah, yeah. Good call." He loaded a tent and a few sleeping bags then went in the house.

Jennie and April were sitting restlessly in front of the TV, where the fire in the next town was gathering more and more attention. A helicopter flew over the Orchard, and a nasty hot wind blew up the creek.

"I should go home," April said. "That's where Yarrow will go."

"If you can get there now," Lou said. "There's embers falling on the cabins."

"Dad, Dad, look!" Jennie screamed.

The fire was coming straight up the creek bed, a hundred yards away.

The sound on the TV was subsumed in a terrible roaring. Flames shot up into the oak tree canopy. The trees exploded, sending sparks ahead of the fire, drifting in the wind onto their deck.

"Get in the truck."

Lou grabbed his keys and the three made a run for it. Lou turned left out of the parking lot, onto the lane that ran deeper into the Orchard.

"What..." April said.

"We've got to tell everyone."

They drove quickly through the Orchard, yelling warnings at each cabin.

Freddie and Tommie came running out, and Tommie screamed, "Where's Frederick? You just had him."

The fire had blown down behind Freddie's cabin, and the scalding heat penetrated the body of Lou's truck. Then Lou and April heard a high-pitched bark from behind a burning shed.

"We can't leave till we find Frederick," Tommie said.

"Take your family and go," Freddie said.

Frederick barked sharply three times.

"Oh, you bad boy, come here right now," Freddie shouted, stamping his foot in frustration. "He's scared. I'm going for him."

Tommie ran into the house and came out with the long leather coat. "Here, take my heavy coat, you brave boy. Here are the keys. I'll wait."

"No, you silly fool. Get in the truck."

"I'm waiting till hell freezes over."

"Tommie, get in the truck," Lou cried. "We have to go."

"Never," Tommie replied. "We can use my car. You go, you go now."

Lou and April finished alerting the residents as the fire raged around them.

Then they drove out of the Orchard. The flames had come down fast, to the residences in the few blocks between the Orchard and the main road. Cars parked at houses and in the roadway were burning. Loud pops and explosions came from the houses. Lou smelled burning plastic.

"Shit, what are we going to do?" April asked. A fifty-foot wall of flames blocked their way.

Lou looked behind him, down the road. Black and brown smoke completely blocked their way. "Drive down the middle of the road."

"How far do we have to go like that?" Jennie asked.

"That's why we're praying," April said. "I love you both."

"Thanks, Mom," Jennie said. "Love you too."

"What did you say?" April asked.

"Roll up the windows," Lou said. The truck entered the fifty-foot flames.

Chapter 39

After the Fire: Where's Yarrow?

Following the hand motions of a blue-clad EMT, Lou rolled his truck slowly onto the football field at the community college. The late summer sun and the drought had burnt the grass to a crisp.

"Shit, the truck smells horrible," Jennie said.

"Burnt, like half the town," April said. "Where's Yarrow? Where is he?"

"I told you, tryouts for the mountain bike team," Jennie replied.

"Back down, Jennie. This is serious," Lou said. They sat in the truck, waiting for someone to tell them where to park.

"I hope he saw the smoke," April said.

"You know Yarrow," Jennie said.

April tapped her phone on her leg again. "Nothing, nothing. Where is he?"

"I have smoke masks in the back," Lou said. "Does anyone want one?"

Ambulances and emergency vehicles circled in the streets outside the field. Siren sounds came from all directions. Cars full of people poured through the field entrance. Two policemen used shrill whistles to direct traffic.

Lou, April and Jennie started to set up the family-sized tent from the back of the truck. People all around them were shouting and crying. One woman sat in a folding chair and stared at her husband, who was struggling to erect their tent in the insistent, dry wind. Thick smoke blew across the field and obliterated the rows of RVs and tents.

"You can't put your tent up there," said a stout woman in a Red Cross vest. "That's the animal shelter area."

"We've moved three times now," Lou said. "Who's running the camp?"

"See this red vest I'm wearing? Your phone won't work,

155

ma'am. The cell towers are burnt or overloaded."

"I know that. My son is missing, goddamn it."

"And our neighbors and their dog," Lou said.

"We have several missing humans. You can file a report once we set up the protocol table."

Lou and Jennie helped Casey set up a tent he'd gotten from a huge pile. Smoke rolled back over the field. Both Lou and April started coughing, and April put on a mask. An ambulance moved cautiously up the temporary street right by Lou's tent. The light started failing as the sun set in a dense cloud of smog. An elderly Hispanic woman talking to the woman with the clipboard burst into tears. The woman handed her a handful of smoke masks.

"Crap," Lou said when the dry wind blew his rain fly across the field. Jennie went to get it. The ambulance sounds were making him crazy. He felt like he was coming out of his skin from an adrenalin overload.

A blond woman with perfectly coifed hair approached him. The temporary lights which had been erected on poles illuminated the hellish scene by his tent, which blew sideways in the hot draft. A woman next door was moaning in Spanish from a bad burn and her husband was drunk. On the other side of Lou's tent two large, black German shepherds barked incessantly.

"Excuse me, sir," a tall man said to Lou. He held a portable TV camera.

"Would you put that fucking thing down and help me?" Lou asked. April had wandered out into the street by the field, trying to pick up a cell signal.

"Sir, our audience wants to know how the people at the evacuation center feel," the blond reporter said.

"Are you broadcasting?"

"Yes, we're live from the community college, where emergency vehicles are…"

Lou interrupted her. "How I feel?"

"Yes." The blond woman turned a wide smile towards the camera, then leaned into him with her large mike.

"Fuck you. Our kid is missing. Either help or get out of the way."

The blond lady turned towards the camera man and touched the little speaker in her ear. "Yes. Tempers are frayed here at the evac center. We'll break for…"

"Where's Yarrow?" April kept saying this over and over. Now she pounded in tent stakes and shouted in time with the fierce hammer blows. "Where, where, where?"

After they secured the tent, April waited with Lou and Jennie by the entrance to the evac center. Other groups of people—couples and individuals—stood anxiously in the smoke and dust at the entrance. Lou noticed that he was rapidly oscillating between gut-wrenching anxiety and a mysterious calm, a new sensation, maybe since he'd seen Angela at her ranch.

As he stood by the gate, waiting for Yarrow and Tommie and Freddie to arrive, something inside of him let down. There was nothing he could do. He could breathe and wait.

He thought *Angela was right. We each have a personal Armageddon every day, but can we be at peace with that fact? Everything coming to an end.* He was glad he'd gone to see her, even though he hadn't gotten the money she owed him.

A man touched his shoulder and interrupted his musing. "Lou?" a man asked. "I'm Bernie's dad."

"Of course," April said.

"They went to practice together," a thin blond woman said. "I can't…"

Tommie came to them through the gloom and smoke, like a huge ghost. He sobbed, "Where's Freddie? Where's my boy, my lovely boy?"

"How did you get out?" Lou asked, hugging him. "We were so worried."

April clung to Tommie. They cried together until they both started coughing.

"Here's a mask, Tommie," Lou said. He had kept several in his jeans pocket.

"Where is he?" April kept saying. She clutched Lou's hand until it hurt. Tommie stood with them for a few moments, then disappeared in the smoke.

"He's a smart kid," Lou said.

"Sometimes," April said.

Bernie's parents turned away and fell silent. A small blond girl holding a teddy bear shuffled her feet and stood next to them.

Time passed strangely for Lou. Everything happened at once

and yet took so long. He helped a woman with two small kids set up a tent, then went back to the gate.

The parking lot and football field were full. Dogs started barking and the sound spread up and down the awkward rows of cars and tents. From time to time, blankets of smelly smoke covered the field, setting off hacking coughs all around Lou. His mask was hot and uncomfortable, so he took it off.

Evening turned into night, which went on forever. A truck pulled into the field full of furniture. Three young boys clung to the back rails. The ambulances had quieted down and some of the evacuees were sleeping. A young man and woman were yelling at each other as they tried to level their camper.

"Come on, Yarrow," April said over and over.

In the distance, down the street, Lou saw a mountain bike coming, with two boys on it, weaving between the police cars, through the pole lights which had been set up.

"There he is." Lou felt a shudder of relief, almost tears.

"I knew he'd make it," Jennie said. Her voice caught in her throat, and the sound surprised Lou.

"Yarrow, oh my god. Are you all right? Let me look at you." Bernie and Yarrow lay the bike down. April grabbed Yarrow and hugged him.

"Can I get a drink?"

Yarrow pulled away from April and slapped hands with Bernie.

Bernie said, "You're so the man. Here's my parents."

Bernie's parents pulled him into a family hug. His sister held the bear doll around her brother's legs.

"What happened to the other bike?" April asked.

Yarrow gulped from a water bottle and said, "Bernie and I were way ahead of the rest of the JV team, killing it. Then the fire came up behind us..."

Bernie's family came over, and his mother said, "Tell us what happened, Bernie."

"When the fire came at us, my bike crashed. Yarrow gave me his and started running with me. We took turns on the bike. We went uphill for a long time. The fire crackled in the trees all around us. Sometimes it cut us off from the trail and we went cross-country, carrying the bike, till we found another single track. I just followed Yarrow. He knew what to do."

Bernie's father shook Yarrow's hand and said, "Thanks, son. Thank you."

A gash on Bernie's shin left a wide red stain on his sock. "Dad, I need some more water."

"And bandages," his mother said. "Thank you so much."

"I have some in my truck," Lou said. "Water, too."

"I'll get them," Jennie said.

Bernie's father reached into his pocket and pulled out his wallet. He offered two hundred dollars to Yarrow. "Please, let us thank you, Yarrow."

"No, thank you, Mr. Barnes," he said. "Bernie and I are friends."

After Bernie and his parents left, Yarrow said, "I did like you said, Lou. I put my head down and did the next thing. The fire was so close, it singed the bike. We carried it and ran alongside all the way, together."

"Yarrow, you're a hero," April said.

"Mom, don't hug me, okay? And please stop crying."

"You did well, Yarrow," Lou said.

"We have clothes for you, Yarrow." April gathered herself. "You need to clean up."

Yarrow looked around at the smoky grounds, the cars and trucks pulling in, people crying and yelling instructions.

"Are we staying here? We have friends in…"

"We're going to help. Now sponge off and go find someone who's putting up a tent."

"Guess you don't stay a hero for long," Yarrow said, carrying fresh clothes and wandering off in the smoky, gloomy glow from the stadium lights, towards the gym.

Jennie was sobbing quietly, standing by the truck holding a bottle of water.

Chapter 40

Freddie and Frederick the Great Are Still Missing

In Lou's dream, water falls on him in torrents. Jennie runs with him towards a burning truck. The ground trembles and begins to fall away. His mother holds out her hand to him. His father is yelling something.

He woke up with April shaking him. "Lou, Lou."

"Wha…"

"You were screaming, 'I can't take it, take it.'"

"Okay. I hate this dream." He felt groggy and lay in bed for a few minutes. "At least you're here with me."

April snuggled into his sleeping bag. "Somehow, it's our dream now."

"I don't know, but I think it's getting better." He felt comforted by April's body curled against him. His racing heart slowed down.

The morning scene outside his tent looked like hell. Bright lights from an occasional car cut through the residual smoke. Dust and ash filled the air. Emergency vehicles in the street nearby still flashed their revolving warning lights.

Breakfast in the college gym was cold cereal, with volunteers shouting orders and looking confused.

April, Yarrow and Jennie joined him a few minutes later.

"Can't sleep with all the noise," Jennie said.

"Why exactly are we here?" Yarrow spooned his oatmeal but didn't eat it. "Smells like shit from all the animals. We can go to my dad's. He offered, you know. We'd at least have warm food."

"Your dad," April said. She looked at Lou.

"I see a lot for us to do here to help. In a few days, we can go to my house."

April raised her eyebrow.

"Come on, Yarrow," Jennie said. "We can go look around."

"Stay out of…"

"Okay, Mom," Yarrow interrupted.

"Everyone is nervous," April said. "I never lost everything before."

"I'm still here." Lou smiled and drank his coffee. For a moment, he could relax. He could focus. He could work all day helping set up the evac center.

In the gym, volunteers in the portable kitchen served up coffee and oatmeal. People gathered in little clumps to eat. Others looked for the names of loved ones on big white boards covered with missing persons reports.

"The road to my house will be cleared tomorrow, maybe. They say."

"Who's they?" April laughed.

"Am I the answer man?" Lou asked, reaching across the table and taking her hand. "In the Orchard, it looks like we'll have water but no gas or electricity. We can cook on the wood stove. Do you want to come? Does Yarrow?"

"What did I tell you about living together? Not until we're committed."

"Isn't there a special coda if your house is burned down?"

"My ex is a lawyer. I'll consult him."

"I mean it," Lou said. "Come and stay."

"We'll see. This is the worst coffee I ever had."

Suddenly his morning calm evaporated.

"This gym right now, this is hellish," Lou said. "Everything is slipping away, my work, my town."

"Your independence?"

"I don't know where to go, what to do next. It's like the fire took everything that makes me sane."

"I know what that's like," April said. "I have no clean underwear."

"At least we're all safe." Lou took a deep breath. "We're all safe."

"I don't feel safe."

Casey sat down at their table. "Is the oatmeal hot yet? Rumors say the fire started at Angela's compound."

"Her own personal Apocalypse," April said. "Has anyone seen her since the fire?"

"No," Casey answered. "Her students are frantic. But there's only one reported death so far. The Christian lady from our

162

neighborhood."

"Jesus came for her," April said.

"Don't be cruel. Do you want to burn to death?" Casey said.

"I heard you die from lack of oxygen first, and it goes pretty quick."

"Ugh, Lou," April said.

"Here comes Tommie. Let's change the topic."

They had stayed up late with him the night before.

"My brave boy went into the fire," Tommie said. He sat down with his coffee. "Who would have picked him to be so brave? And foolhardy? Now both my Freddies are missing."

Tommie put his head down on his massive arms next to his coffee cup and began weeping. "I cannot take any more grief. I can't. I just want to see him again, please, please. I don't believe in god, but now I need him. I can't go through this again."

Tommie picked his head up. "I need to be strong. I need to look for him. Lou, will you come with me?"

Tommie and Lou wandered through the tent village. "Please look around for my brave boy, Lou. I can't see through all the tears in my eyes."

Lou took Tommie's arm and steered him through the uneven rows of tents. Some people were setting up tents, while others were taking them down and moving on.

Jennie walked up to them a few minutes later, carrying Frederick the Great. "Look what..."

Tommie let out a scream and swept up Jennie and the dog in a massive hug. Frederick the Great started yapping and slobbering on Tommie.

"Frederick, how did you get here? You bad boy. Now, where is our Freddie? You brought him, didn't you? Do you want some water, some food? I'm sure you want some water. Oh, you love bug, you love child, you. Oh, Jennie, you're so..."

"I haven't seen Freddie. I'm so sorry," Jennie said. "We found Frederick by the gate."

Tommie burst into tears.

The threesome went over to the gymnasium, where there were bags of donated dog food. Casey met them as they looked for a bowl. "I hate to say it. They found a man's body near our neighborhood."

"No," Tommie wailed.

As they looked at a card on the white board, a woman in a red vest came over and took down the card.

"Oh, were you looking at this? This poor man was found on the other side of the fire. It's so hard to keep everything straight." She wrote on the card and replaced it.

"Can't be him, can't be him," Tommie said. "Frederick the Great made it."

Casey, Lou and Tommie sat down at a nearby table and watched the families and individuals walking around, looking for loved ones, or word of them. Emergency phone numbers were pinned up on another wall but cell service wasn't up yet. Engineers were installing a bank of land lines.

The lady in the red vest came back. "I have to correct this card again," she said. "Sorry. So much information."

Tommie read it out loud. "In the woods near town, near the Orchard. What is that? A long leather coat, no identification. A small man." He looked at Lou and said, "It's him. It's him. I just knew it couldn't last."

Chapter 41

Resolution

As the sun rose, the tent village appeared out of the low, smoky fog. Lou went over to the impromptu kitchen to begin Day Two. The terror was beginning to leave his muscles and he stretched as he walked.

"Fire. It's the scariest thing in the world," he said. He took a deep breath and relaxed.

"Worse than your dream?" April laughed.

"I've been sleeping a little better since…"

"Angela?"

"I hate to think so."

April laughed. She put a fork into her eggs. "Not sure this is edible."

"We can make food on my camp stove," Lou said. "And some real coffee."

"That sounds good." April looked around. "I'm torn between getting some support myself and trying to help," she said.

"What's new about that?"

"Now who's the counselor? You don't know how important having a house is till you can't go there. Or, I know it sounds funny, how important Yarrow is until I thought he might be dead. Rootlessness is kind of liberating. Anything can happen and everything is so immediate. That thin veil of stability is gone. I can see why it could be attractive to you."

"No shit. For me, that veil is quite insubstantial."

"Unstable," April added and smiled.

"It can go too far."

Lou looked around the big cafeteria room. Casey raised his mug at a nearby table, where he sat with Mrs. Goodwin. Aaron rolled up to them in his new wheelchair.

"I keep thinking about my storage sheds. Art I can't make again."

"Everybody lost something. You still have a house."

"I know. I got lucky. There's still slabs of wood and animals to carve."

Tears filled April's eyes. "The school is gone. Our home is gone. So much for the five-minute evacuation drill. I never went home. I have no idea where to start."

Lou leaned across the table towards her. "We'll figure something out."

"We?"

"How am I going to work? Home-school Jennie? I don't know."

"The school is going to start up in temporary buildings, they said."

"I wish I had a dollar for every 'they said' that never happened."

"That's why they call it an emergency."

"The kids are still sleeping?"

"When I left."

The evacuated townspeople had set up their tents in little family units and neighborhoods on the football field. Casey's tent was nearby. The first night, April, Yarrow, Jennie and Lou had slept in his big camping tent, on donated blankets. Then April had time to go out and buy her own.

Later that morning, Lou sat in a donated beach chair and drank donated coffee. The smoke irritated his eyes. He was used to getting up and going to work, but the town had shut down. If he ever had a reason to leave Bingo, this was it.

There was nothing to do now. He had spent the previous day helping people park their cars and trucks in straight rows, put up tents, and secure their animals. He had worked inside the gym setting up chairs and tables, and running pipes for the temporary kitchen.

Today he could sit for a few minutes, watching the other evacuees coming out of their tents, looking around at their piles of donated clothes and water. The volunteer coordinator would find him and give him projects. He took a deep breath. More of the anxiety was leaving his body.

Casey joined him on the donated chairs. He rubbed his head and said, "Plenty of work for a volunteer grief counselor. This one guy yesterday told me that he got his kids and wife in the truck and they all got out. Then he started sobbing about his lost German Shepherd. That was one of twenty conversations yesterday."

"How are you?"

"I don't know. I miss Lily pretty bad. When I wake up, I think, Well, where is that … fill in the blank … photo, license, memento. And then I remember. No mas."

"It's a brutal way to find out what's really important."

"That's halfway to a better question, 'Who am I?' Right now, before coffee, I don't want to know."

"I'll go get you some."

"Do I look like an invalid? I'll get it. When I leave here, where do I go? An empty piece of land by the creek. Johnie will probably want rent money."

"It's so weird that my house is still there and Freddie is dead. Not a quarter-mile away."

"You tried to save him. Would you go back for a dog? What a joke."

"Don't say that around a dog lover."

"With Lily dead, I asked myself, 'Why am I still alive?' And now the fire." Casey drank his coffee. "It's a good time for you to leave, of course."

"I've still got a house and the survivor guilt that goes with it."

"You're not sensitive enough for that." Casey laughed. "I mean, you've survived so much. You don't talk about it but I know. I could fall asleep right here, in the sun, nice chair. But I can't sleep. When I close my eyes, I see the fire in my hallway and I'm looking for Lily's ashes." He looked up at the distant hills through the lightly smoky air. "The bible was right."

"Don't say it."

"Ashes to ashes. I gotta go for a walk and move these old bones. Coming?"

"No, thanks. I'll sit here and watch the world go by."

April came across the wide field, carrying an armload of newspapers, which she handed to other refugees who sat by their tents in fold-up chairs. She had a smile and a short word with each one.

He liked the graceful way she touched other people when she gave them a paper. He could feel the generosity of soul in her, the

167

way she talked to those who were in trouble. All of a sudden, he took a deep breath and relaxed. Life felt good.

As she came back to their tents, Yarrow and Jennie emerged from their respective tents.

"Hey, Mom. We could have gone…"

"Hush now. Maybe one more day. Do you really want to go to your father's?"

"No."

"I told you. We can help. Maybe you could learn a little about…" April sat down next to Lou. "Shit, I don't know. Go get some breakfast."

"I'm so bored. Let me know if something happens." Yarrow turned to Jennie. "Coming?" They strolled across the field, each carrying a skateboard.

April and Lou drank their coffee.

"You didn't tell him that you wanted to stay here with me," Lou said with a smile.

"Didn't I?"

"You could have…"

"This is still the worst coffee," she said, as she put her index finger into her cup and flicked some at Lou.

"What are you going to do today?" Lou asked.

April didn't answer. She was looking at her phone.

As the fog lifted a little over the grounds of the civic center, Lou felt calm again, with April next to him. He knew that it might not last. But there it was.

He looked down the rows of tents, towards the people of Bingo. Maybe he could stay and help. Maybe he was tired of helping.

But he had his house. No work. For a moment, he felt heavy and sorrowful, for all the loss and disruption the people in the tents had felt and would feel. It was like he was the whole town for a moment, with this vast burn running through the middle of his heart.

He choked up, and wondered about his new-found vulnerability. April made appointments with the mothers of her students.

Without April, he didn't think he could live happily again. The realization shocked him.

"Hey, are you all right?" April asked.

Lou looked far off, into the distant hills. He felt calm again.

"Why don't you stay with me?"

"We've talked about that. I mean, I talked and you listened. I can't do that to myself, or to Yarrow..."

"I'm staying. I want to help rebuild Bingo."

"Heroic," April said.

"Don't be a tough chick now," Lou said. "I want you and Yarrow to help me find a new house, for all of us. Away from the Orchard. I want you."

"You know what living with you means, right?"

"Absolutely. White picket fence. White dress. It could be yours."

"Add white couples and you got the Aryan Nation."

"I'm serious."

April looked at him and then took his hand.

Suddenly, Lou's chest filled with heat. He felt like crying, like shouting. He stood up and gave April a hug. "I feel so hot, so big, so wild, so in love," he said. "I'm staying in Bingo and you're staying with me."

"Finally," she said, hugging him back.

Chapter 42

The Devil Made Me Do It

"Half the town is gone but we're still here," Lou said. He and April were bunking, waking up in Lou's living room, in a new bed they'd bought. Yarrow was sleeping on the deck, at least until the first rain, or until they found a bigger house. It was their first night back from the football field, and a faint odor of smoke hung over Bingo.

"I like being here," April said. "But not being able to go home is super-strange. Like, what am I doing living with my boyfriend?"

"I can fix that."

"What?"

Lou rolled out of their mattress on the floor and grabbed a small box off a coffee table. He knelt next to April and asked, "Will you marry me?"

April started to cry. She sat up and opened the box. A brilliant tiny diamond set into five little golden leaves caught her attention.

"Lou, it's so you."

"It's so us?"

"Yes, yes." She threw her arms around him and they fell back into bed, hugging.

Jennie came out of her room. "Sounded like something fell..."

"We're okay." April looked at Lou.

"I asked April to marry me."

"You didn't ask me if it would be all right?"

"Maybe I skipped a step." Lou tried to read Jennie's sober expression.

"I can live with it. Do we have any eggs?"

"I'll make some," April said. "I gotta get dressed."

"You look rustic and cute standing there at the stove," Lou said a few minutes later. "I could get used to that. Get you an apron…"

"We need to talk," April said. She stirred the eggs. "I keep thinking about the folks who are still at the evac center."

"Okay," Lou said.

"I don't have time to go and help them."

"Well, yeah. You're setting up a whole new school."

Jennie ate her eggs with a fork. "I really liked that owl you carved, Dad," she said. "I'm sorry it burned up in the shop. I was hoping it would eat the rodents you left under my bed."

"There's plenty of owls around," Lou said.

The day went by quickly. Looking through the burned-out shop for salvageable tools, doing the laundry, buying a new air mattress for Yarrow. Half the people in town were looking for housing, like they were. Night fell, still accompanied by the smell of smoke.

"Lou, wake up. You're having another nightmare."

Lou became aware of April shaking him. He pulled himself awake.

"Shit," he moaned. But after a few minutes of watching his breath, he went back to sleep. Then he smelled smoke and thought he was still dreaming.

Till Jennie screamed. Flames were shooting up around the deck outside the window.

"Dad, Dad!"

"Get out," Lou yelled at April. "Get out." She rolled over and ran for the door, then stopped. "Yarrow is out on the deck." Lou ran through the thick smoke and fell over his couch. "Shit."

He pulled Jennie out of her room as the doorway to the bedroom collapsed behind him. He half carried and half dragged her outside as the fire overwhelmed the living room. Both of them fell on the ground outside, choking and coughing.

The redwood walls and roof caught and burned quickly.

Lou couldn't believe it. Everyone was shouting and the fire was roaring in his ears. Now he heard multiple sirens.

Someone was screaming on the other side of the house.

How could his house be on fire?

Wood flames crackled and the deck fell through.

Yarrow came around the house. He staggered and fell.

"Yarrow, you're bleeding," April said. Lou put his arm

around him. Streams of blood dripped off his head and stained his white tee shirt.

"Were you burning something on the deck?" Lou asked.

Who was that screaming? Lou wondered. The sirens got closer and closer.

"No. Hell no. I saved your asses. That weird stalker guy fell over me when I was sleeping. He spilled gasoline on me. When I got up, he said, 'Shit, looks like I have to burn you, too.' Then he tried to light some more matches and I jumped on him. We fell off the deck. Somehow I bumped my head."

"That's quite a bump," Lou said. "The paramedics are almost here."

The four of them stood together, as the fire engines got closer and closer.

"Dad," Jennie said, pointing. "Look."

Luke stood in the middle of the driveway, trying to block the fire engines. He waved an empty gasoline can. "The devil made me do it. The devil made me do it," he yelled repeatedly. "Let it burn." He danced in front of the fire engines till a policeman pulled him out of the way. Luke took a swing at him. It took three officers to pin him down. The fireman jumped off the truck and attached their hose to a water main.

Luke kept yelling, "Let it burn. Let it burn," as the police led him away in hand cuffs. He looked back at Jennie and said, "I'll take you to Oregon when I get back."

Yarrow said, "Man, I really hate fires."

Jennie said, "I hate the evac center. I'm not going back."

"We're a family. We'll figure something out," Lou added.

Lou watched the firemen unroll their hoses. Streams of water showered onto the cabin and intermingled with the towering yellow-gold flames. Suddenly the roof of the cabin collapsed. A blast of heat and light blew out of the house and across the deck. Wicker chairs tore through the railing, as the whole side of the house disappeared in the white-hot inferno.

George M. Taylor was born in Detroit, Michigan and graduated from the University of Michigan. He moved to Northern California, where he has lived in many towns. This is his first novel.